The Boy on CINNAMON STREET

By PHOEBE STONE

SCHOLASTIC INC.

To David, who rescued me.

ISBN 978-0-545-21828-3

Arthur A. Levine Books hardcover edition designed by Whitney Lyle, published by Arthur A. Levine Books, an imprint of Scholastic Inc., February 2012.

12 11 10 9 8 7 6 5 4 3 2 1   13 14 15 16 17 18/0

Printed in the U.S.A.   40

This edition first printing, May 2013

Prologue

My name used to be Louise but it's not anymore. I had a T-shirt made that says across the front NO LONGER LOUISE. I changed my name because Louise rhymes with cheese and fleas and sneeze. So now I'm Thumbelina. I know. I know. It's over the top. It's unrealistic. It's childish and stupid. Nobody has that name. But the thing is, I'm little. I'm only four feet seven and I'm in seventh grade. This means I have a seventh-grade soul that's stuck in a fourth-grade body. This is major annoying. I'm planning on growing taller soon.

I came up with the idea of Thumbelina when I was walking along the river with my friend Henderson. He was looking at the sky. Henderson always looks at the sky when he's thinking and he's *always* thinking. He was saying, "Actually everybody has a story, a fairy tale in their heart that they adhere to. That's why Hans Christian Andersen is so awesome."

"Adhere to?" I said. This is the way this kid talks, seriously. Then I started looking up at the sky with Henderson. He's very tall and I'm very small, and people started honking at us because it looked like we might wander into the half-frozen river by mistake. But while I was cloud watching with Henderson, it came to me. I "adhere to" the story of Thumbelina.

That was around the time in my life that things started shifting, like slabs of ice on a river. It all began with a very very snowy winter and a pizza I ordered after my grandma had a yard sale. I think of that pizza now as a cosmic wheel spinning through the universe, changing everything.

Chapter One

Through the window, I can see South Pottsboro is frozen solid. It's icy and windy out there. In this case the word *south* is misleading. I don't see any palm trees. *Dumpy, boring* Pottsboro would be more accurate. There's another snowstorm on the way and my grandma is having an indoor yard sale in the foyer of our condo building. A yard sale during a snowstorm?

My grandma is like, "Blah blah blah. We're the first people this season to have a sale. We'll be swamped."

My grandpa is all huffy because he doesn't want to put his slippers in the yard sale. He's wearing them to keep them safe, which is totally embarrassing because these slippers look like roadkill. Seriously.

And the lady downstairs already has plenty against my grandpa because he does noisy limbering-up exercises in our living room and then that lady starts pounding on our door. My grandma is very two-faced at these times. She's so sweet to that lady then, but later, in the middle of the night, I can hear my grandma and grandpa laughing and giggling and calling her a big jerk.

In the middle of the night through the walls, I hear my grandma and grandpa talking about other things too. Sometimes they aren't giggling. They're talking about me. Sometimes my grandma starts sobbing and my grandpa goes, "Baby doll, give her a little time. She just needs more time. Relax. Relax." And then the room goes stone silent like they both died in there.

Right now my grandpa and I are going outside to the steps to put up a flyer on the glass front door. It says YARD SALE TODAY: EXERCISE BICYCLE, DISHES, BOOKS,

AND A BALANCE BEAM. Okay. The balance beam is mine. I used to be in gymnastics until about a month ago. Okay. It used to be my life. I spent a million hours a week on that balance beam. I lived on that freaking beam. But it was my idea to sell it.

It's cold out here. My grandpa's scarf (which he calls a muffler) blows around. My grandpa blows around in the wind. When he leans over, a silver letter opener falls out of his pocket onto the snow. "Hey," says my grandpa, "nobody was gonna buy a letter opener anyway. Nobody writes real letters anymore. Right, pal?"

"Whatever, Grandpa," I say. Right now I would like to do a cartwheel, but I don't. This cartwheel feeling wells up in me constantly, the same way my breath comes up out of me. I used to do cartwheels like the way other people say yes or no. Cartwheels used to *be* my yes and my no. From here I can see my balance beam. It's lying there waiting for me to run toward it, waiting for my handsprings and my double twists. I turn away. My grandma was like, "Are you sure you want to sell this, Louise?" I didn't answer her.

Henderson says that hikers freezing to death on Mount Everest don't feel a thing. He says they think they're falling asleep next to a warm fire when actually they're lying in a snowbank, their body temperatures dropping to below zero while they are slowly becoming blocks of ice.

Soon enough the front doors open and a whole herd of revved-up South Pottsboro shoppers pour in. "Bingo!" says my grandma, twinkling at all the customers milling around. I swear my grandma stepped out of *The Wizard of Oz*. This includes the Munchkin vocabulary.

"She's a pro. Your grandma's no space cadet, that's for sure," says my grandpa, swinging his arms around.

Now people start picking up things: my grandpa's ripped magazines, my grandma's sweaters, beat-up rusty pots and pans. There's a row of old shoes under the table and in the lineup I see a pair of my mom's. They're kind of worn to the side and you can see where her toes rested against the soft leather. They're sky blue and each shoe carries with it the shape of my mom's foot and the whole shift and feel of her weight. A little girl is jumping around holding them now because she wants them for her dress-up box. "Okay," says the lady with her. "We'll buy them." When the lady hands my grandma two dollars, my grandma looks down. Her face gets lost and blurry and she holds the shoes in her hands for just a second too long.

I look up now and Mrs. Stevenson is sitting on my balance beam. She's Terry Stevenson's mom. "Sold," she says, glaring at some man who is walking by. "Sold," she says again when he turns around. "How much is the balance beam?" she calls out. "I'd like to buy it for my daughter. You're not part of the team anymore, Louise?" She looks over at me with a blank smiling face, the kind of empty, almost hurt smile other people's mothers always give you, as if they cannot bear to give any part of a real smile to anybody but their own child. I don't answer. I don't feel like answering anybody today.

My balance beam is one of the first things to sell, but it is one of the last things to leave. It sits in the foyer late into the afternoon. Then the snowstorm gets worse and the electricity goes out and it's all shadowy and dark down there. Then it's a good thing that beam is pushed off to the side because anybody could stumble over it in the dark and really get hurt. You could tell how much Mrs. Stevenson wanted that beam because she sends over four high school kids to get it during the worst part of the storm.

Chapter Two

After the yard sale, I decide to order a pizza. This is a no-brainer as I practically live on pizza. Palomeeno's Pizza is very dependable. They would deliver pizza even if there were a tornado in South Pottsboro with roofs flapping around and houses flying off their foundations, like in *The Wizard of Oz*.

For some dumb reason, I am thinking about my mom's sky blue shoes when I place the order on my cell. My dad liked those shoes. They were the kind of shoes you had to follow across the rug because of that color. I can't remember anything else. Zippo. Squat. I'm glad that kid bought those shoes because now I won't have to see that color by mistake when I open a closet door. Lake blue. Pond blue. Dark sky blue.

When the doorbell buzzes, my grandma is there before I am. She's always hoping to nose around and get chatty with some boring dork. My grandpa is right behind her, looking for a chance to barge in on what she's doing. So with a lineup like this, there is no chance I'll even *see* this pizza for a while. I lean against the refrigerator, ho-humming to myself.

My grandma throws the door open, and under normal conditions, an hour later, after we've heard the guy's entire life history, she'll hand me the pizza. But not this time. No, this is different. The door is standing open and my grandma sort of freezes when she sees the delivery kid. Then she crumples against my grandpa and backs away.

"Okay, thank you, son," my grandpa says too loudly. I hate when he calls total strangers *son*. He takes the pizza and hands it to me, saying, "Thank you. Thank you. You got correct change, pal?" He leads my grandma to the couch with his arm around her. I can hear them now murmuring and whispering together in the living room.

I give the kid the money from the pizza money jar. He seems to be about fourteen years old. I think a junior from South drives the pizza van and I'm guessing this kid does the running around. To me he doesn't look like a serial killer. He looks all happy in a pizza delivery dude sort of way because he found the place easily, didn't get lost, and isn't having any trouble getting paid. The pizza smells promising. It's the perfect thing to order during a snowstorm after you have just sold the most important thing in your life. Ha ha.

I look again at the kid in the cheerful red jacket with the pizza name tag on the pocket. I look at his face and suddenly out of nowhere I feel like I'm falling or sliding. Henderson saw this film taken on Mount Everest and this woman climber forgot to hitch back on to the rope and she went flying off the mountain a million miles an hour, grabbing at the snow. They filmed her falling. The thing is, after that, the other hikers had to keep on going, trying to get to the summit.

I take the pizza box. It feels so warm. It smells so hopeful. By the time I get to the living room and flop down on the couch and open the lid, my grandma and grandpa are fully recovered from whatever it was. My grandpa, as usual, is being a couch hog. But still, my grandma looks at me and says, "You okay? Everything all right, sweetie? That pizza looks delicious!" which is weird and getting weirder because my grandma hates pizza.

My grandpa reaches for a slice. My grandma frowns. "What?" he says, looking down at his old slippers. "They're comfortable. Who cares what they look like?"

"Men. I'm not talking about the slippers," says my grandma, taking the slice of pizza out of his hand and putting it back in the box. "You're having wild salmon for dinner."

"Grrr," says Grandpa. "Watch out for me. I'm a party animal." He tightens his arm around my grandma and nuzzles against her. She's wearing her green organic sweatshirt that says, I'M ECO MEAN AND GLOBAL GREEN. And she's got Grandpa squeezed into one that's too tight for him and has a hood, which he's wearing now. It makes him look like a big pizza-stealing elf.

"By the way, pal," says my grandpa, "there's a note for you sticking out from under the doormat in the hall." He puts his arm around me too and then he says, "Two beautiful dolls and I'm here in the middle. I call that luck."

"Grandpa, you're sitting on my skirt. I can't get up," I say, pushing him away.

Out in the hall, I look down at the wool doormat. It has a picture of a sheep featured on it and below it says, WOOLCOME HOME. I see the white paper poking out from one of the corners. I know the routine. How many of these letters and notes did I used to get from Merit Madson? Every time I turned around, I would find another. And what did they say? Oh, cute little things like *Quit the gymnastics team or your toast.* (It should have been "you're toast," but Merit Madson can't spell.)

Last month I felt something in my boot, something scratching my ankle. I reached down and pulled out a freaking letter from Merit Freaking Madson. It said something really encouraging about me finding another after-school sport.

I do see the note, but I don't want to pick it up. On the other hand, I don't want my grandpa to read it. Since he's been retired, my grandma says, he has nothing to do but nose around in other people's business. *My* business. So I reach for the note and open the folded paper.

I look down at it and read, *I am your biggest fan.* I reread it to make sure I got it right. I did. It says clearly, *I am your biggest fan.*

What? I mean, seriously, what?

My grandpa comes to the open door and so does my grandma. They look like Mr. and Mrs. Mouse with these curious eyes peering out at me. I'm not your baby mouse, Grandpa. I don't eat corn like you do and I want to go back to Cinnamon Street and live there. Alone.

"Louise?" says my grandma.

"I'm not Louise anymore. I changed my name," I say and I push by them and go in my room and slam the door.

Outside my window, the snowstorm is whirling and raging like white anger and when I push my face against the glass, I can see millions and billions of snowflakes dancing and diving past my window. Henderson says snowflakes are little universes unto themselves. Each snowflake a little world different from all the others. And then he tells me to stick my head out into a snowstorm and look straight up, to understand *everything*. This is how he talks, I'm not kidding you. I think about the pizza delivery guy again. In my mind I look at the name tag on his jacket. It says Benny McCartney. Did Benny McCartney leave me the note? Does Benny McCartney *like* me? Or has there been some kind of cosmic mix-up, some kind of mistake, a big mistake, like forgetting to hitch back on to a rope when you're halfway up Mount Everest in the middle of winter.

Chapter Three

"Duh, I must be brain-dead," I say to my friend Reni on the phone. "I don't understand this note. I'm totally spooked about it. I feel like I just arrived from planet Ha Ha The Joke's On Me."

"Duh, I must be brain-dead too," says Reni. "So let's go be brain-dead losers together and stuff ourselves with ice cream at Ben & Jerry's. Then you can show me the note and we can get Henderson to put it under a microscope and analyze the handwriting. He'll be able to tell you who wrote it. Possibly."

"Okay, I'll meet you there," I say. Reni's the best. She and Henderson are the only friends that I have in the entire universe. That includes all the millions and billions of solar systems and all the trillions and jillions of light-years and black holes and meteor showers that Henderson loves to talk about.

I get on the Toot Toot Tourist Trolley and find a seat along the aisle facing out. The toot toot part was my grandpa's idea. It was supposed to attract droves of tourists. So far it hasn't worked. I look out the window across the aisle from me, watching South Pottsboro flash by. I put my hand in my pocket. I can feel the papery edge of the letter I got last night. I pull it out and look at it, keeping the corners folded so no one can see it. I study the way the words sit on the page, the way the pen looped across the paper

At my stop I put the note away and get off the trolley.

Now I'm in Middle Pottsboro, headed for Ben & Jerry's. I have to climb over a pile of snow at the edge of the street that's about as high as Mount Everest. Snow is piled along the sidewalks and this is March, I'm not kidding you. Everybody is like, "Whoa, more snow?" I can't believe Ben & Jerry's has a huge long line going out the door even though it's snowing. Through the crowds, I spot Reni.

"Reni. Reni. Reni," I call out. She smiles. Her full name is Irene Nancy Elliot and she's five feet eight. I didn't know her when I went to North last year. I know her from when she took an after-school gymnastics class for weight loss at South this year. I was a team leader for that class. I had her doing all kinds of cartwheels right away. Now to get Reni going sometimes, I put up my fists and start jumping around her, saying, "Come on, Reni, put 'em up. Put 'em up." And I start boxing and punching at the air in front of her. Because I'm only four feet seven, she looks *way* down at me sweetly and starts laughing. This always makes her laugh.

I cut into the line headed toward Reni. She has just made it inside. As soon as I get to her, we both start jumping up and down and screaming. Reni started it. "I can't believe you got that note. It's so sweet. You're so lucky. Wow," goes Reni.

I've been jumping up and down with her but I'm not sure why. "I am?" I say.

"Yes," says Reni. She smiles. She has a truly lovely smile; even my grandma says so. Her whole face just lights up like fireworks with extra flashes falling away into the darkness. "Let me see the note," she says.

So I reach in my pocket and get out the crumpled piece of paper with the words *I am your biggest fan* written on it. We both stare down at it. Some lady from planet Extremely Nosy standing next to Reni tries to read it, so Reni turns around and forms a serious Reni wall. "Is this for real?" Reni goes. "I mean, do you know this guy Benny McCartney?"

"I don't think so," I say. "Possibly my grandma knows him, but I'm not sure. I mean, I thought he had just started on the job. I don't think he's delivered any pizza to our condo before, but maybe I just didn't notice."

"You didn't notice him? This guy is major in love with you and you don't notice him?" says Reni. "Think about it. How could you miss something like this? I mean, this could be your ticket to the Spring Fling Dance."

We're near the large windows along the front now and I can see it's starting to snow again. Through the blur of steam and the crowds waiting in line, I can see my only-other-friend-in-the-world Henderson (Reni's brother). He's wearing a sandwich board for Ben & Jerry's. On both sides of the board it says in big letters, DON'T GO AWAY, IT'S FREE CONE DAY. Even though it's cold out there, it looks like Henderson is having a good time walking back and forth. This kid always has a good time, even when he's taking tests at school. Finally he looks through the large window in front and waves to us.

"What is he doing?" I say.

"Oh, he gets these after-school jobs here and there. I don't know. I think he's friends with the manager. He knows everybody and he's always doing dumb things."

"Yeah," I say.

"Henderson is such a pain. You're sooo lucky you don't have a brother," says Reni.

Then Henderson opens the door at Ben & Jerry's and walks in smiling. He's one of these kids who smiles when there is nothing to smile about, which, to use his favorite word, is baffling.

Everybody, including the manager, beams at the sandwich board and at the very tall goofball inside it. Some girls come over to chat with Henderson. Some knock on the front of the sandwich board, trying to be funny.

After ten billion years, Reni and I finally get our ice cream. Now the sandwich board walks toward our table. He has a wool scarf wrapped around his neck and there are snowflakes still on the scarf, and stars of snow stuck to his pointed red wool hat.

"Guess what?" says Reni, throwing open her arms. "*She* got a love letter."

"Really?" Henderson says. "Wow!" He does a couple of jumping jacks inside the sandwich board and then he frowns at both of us through his wire-rimmed glasses.

"We're almost sure who it's from," says Reni.

"Hush," I say, kicking Reni gently with my foot under the table.

"Ouch. We need your help," says Reni.

"Hmmm," says Henderson, crossing his arms over the front of the sandwich board, so now it feels like we're talking to a pack of cards in *Alice in Wonderland.* "Well, Thumb, at least you know someone out there in the universe finds you lovable."

"Not *someone*," says Reni. "Benny McCartney, this cute guy who delivers pizza."

"Oh," says Henderson, backing away.

"And to be sure, we need you to analyze the hand-writing," says Reni.

"Not now. Maybe later," I say, putting my arm on the table to cover the paper.

"Hmmm," says Henderson again. And he grabs my ice-cream cone and I let him take a bite because he's number two in my best-friend lineup.

Then he goes, "I gotta get back to work. It's cold out there but at least it's not Jupiter. On Jupiter you'd freeze *and* choke to death instantly, if you weren't wearing a space suit." He looks cheerfully at us. Then he reaches for Reni's ice cream, but she pulls it away.

"Go get your own," says Reni, "and grow up while you're at it."

Henderson smiles. Seriously, I've never ever seen this kid look sad. He told me once he thinks *everything* in the world is interesting, even boring things. Now he heads toward the door, waving to the manager.

"He's always doing stupid stuff like this," says Reni. "Hey, Henderson, what did you do with Annais's Chinese fan, the one she had on her wall above her desk? It's suddenly missing." But Henderson doesn't hear her. He's already outside in the falling snow, hopping around on the sidewalk and joking with shoppers.

Reni rolls her eyes and shrugs her shoulders. Then suddenly she gets really quiet. She looks at the crumpled paper on the table. "You should be happy. I never got a letter from Justin Bieber, and I wrote him five times. I can understand not answering one letter, but five letters? It's like rejection times five."

"Reni, we don't know if he even got any of the letters."

"True," goes Reni.

"You know what? I feel like I need to know more about Benny McCartney. I have this funny feeling," I say. "And it's kind of, I don't know."

"Uh-oh," goes Reni. "Are you starting to get, like, 'obsessed' with this guy? I mean, are you thinking about him twenty-four seven?"

"Maybe," I say, "sort of."

"Uh-oh," goes Reni, shaking her head. "Sounds like a crush."

And then I start thinking about my grandma and how she kind of backed away when she saw that pizza kid. She didn't go, "Darling, how are you?" like she does to *everybody* she encounters. My grandma gets to know the personal history of every dork she meets. But for this kid, she was all strange and shaky.

"Um, maybe *you* should order a pizza, Reni, and see if he leaves *you* a note. Maybe this kid has cracked up and leaves notes for everybody. Maybe he's, like, a pizza stalker," I say.

"Yeah, but I'm not allowed to order pizza," says Reni, looking down at her T-shirt, where there are two pink spots of bubble gum ice cream. Her T-shirt is a Gap XL and across the front are the printed words LOVE ME ANYWAY? "I never get pizza. I have borderline diabetes. The doctor says I have to lose twenty pounds or I have to go on insulin."

"Now you tell me, Reni. Let's get out of here. Say good-bye *forever* to that friendly Ben & Jerry's cow behind your head." I pull on Reni's arm and she gets up and we start laughing. Then I say again, "Reni, can we find out where Benny McCartney lives at least? He goes to North, I know that."

"I can ask my sister. Annais knows everybody at North. Come on, admit it. This is an unmistakable crushy kissy kind of thing," says Reni.

"I don't know," I say again. My first and only crush passes through my mind. It was on Frosty the Snowman when I was six years old. I know it was stupid, but it came with a sort of warm, fuzzy, longing feeling. "Reni, this doesn't feel good."

"Of course not," says Reni. "Crushes hurt. None of them feel good. They're pure agony."

"Oh," I say.

"Remember when I first starting crushing Justin Bieber? It was major pain."

"Okay," I say. And I feel a little better having given a name to this strange unwanted sliding feeling that seems to be pulling at me. Then Reni starts laughing again and I join in, though I'm not sure why. But Reni and I are really good at laughing. It's all we ever do. Too bad they don't have laughing contests, cause Reni and I would rule.

When we get out to the sidewalk, it's still snowing. It's a dizzying, confusing snow. If you stare up at the snowflakes like Henderson says to do, you lose your balance. You feel like you're floating. You don't know where the sky is and where the ground is. Is this how to understand *everything*?

From where we are standing, we can see Henderson in his sandwich board up on the corner. A group of pigeons have flocked around him and are looking up at him. Henderson is waving his arms around in the snow like he's their conductor, a conductor of a pigeon choir.

"What a doofus," says Reni.

Chapter Four

It's Saturday and my grandma and grandpa are going to yet another antique show. "No way," I say. "Do I have to go? There might be a tornado today. It said so on the Internet. I think I'd rather hang out in the basement to be safe." But the sky is a pure blue. The snow has stopped and Grandpa is all smiley and gives me a hug. He's so excited. He collects old beer bottles. I'm not kidding you. After he finds one, he is like a crazy man singing and kissing my grandma, all over finding some stupid bottle that should have gone in the trash a hundred years ago.

"You need to get out of the house," says my grandma, and she hands me a pair of socks made of recycled materials. They're made from old plastic milk and yogurt containers all smashed up and spun into plastic yarn. They look like regular socks, but they're not. I'll probably just keep thinking about old spilled milk when I'm wearing them.

Grandma puts her arm around me and whispers, "With every step we take, we need to be more aware of our magical green environment."

My calendar says I've got nothing to do, so I go along. My calendar is so blank I can reuse it every year by just flipping a few numbers around. Clever, no? Grandma drives because Grandpa needs new glasses, and the whole way there he's telling her what to do and where to turn and where to go. Every time we come toward a stoplight, Grandpa stomps his foot on the floor on the passenger side, trying to stop the car.

"All right, Mr. Control Freak," Grandma says.

I'm sitting all by myself in the big empty backseat,

thinking about that letter and Benny McCartney. Reni is so excited that I have a crush on somebody. I'm pleased that she's so pleased. It's true I've never been in crush land before (except for Frosty, and I'm just being honest.) All the signposts are upside down and backward here because I don't know what a true crush is supposed to feel like. And then I don't feel anything about certain stuff anyway and this freaks my grandma and grandpa. They go to this dorky support group that I call a big crying festival. They are always trying to get me to go with them. But I won't.

Honestly, I don't feel a thing about my mom or my dad. It's like when a doctor gives you a shot of painkiller for a broken hand or something and you go home and put that hand on a hot burner on the stove by mistake — you could burn up your hand if you aren't looking because you don't feel a thing. Not one thing.

We pull up in front of the antique show. Grandma parks the car nicely and doesn't bump or smash into anything. She smiles at Grandpa and says, "Perfect. What did I tell you?"

And Grandpa says, "You're wedged too close to that truck, baby doll. The guy's gonna come back and dance all over our car. Let me repark this thing."

I'm not in any hurry. I hate antique shows. There's nothing old that I like anyway. Except maybe a little jewelry box that used to belong to my mother. When you open the lid, it plays this little song called "Oh Stars in the Sky."

> Oh stars in the sky,
> All the stars twinkling by,
> I wish and I sigh
> At the stars so high.
> I wish and I sigh
> And I wonder why.
> Why? Why? Why?

My mother pinned a picture of herself, my father, and me on the inside of the lid on the soft white satin. It's still there. When you open the lid, you hear the song and you see the photo.

As we walk into the building and down the rows of

booths full of junk, my grandma gets all excited and says, "Louise, darling, pick something out. Anything at all, dear. For your room." She pats my hair. Her hands smell of rose hand cream. Grandpa and she kind of match. They go together like a set of something, like two canisters on an antique table. That starts me thinking, would Benny and I make a good set of salt and pepper shakers? Seriously.

"Louise," says Grandma, "anything here. I mean it."

I have told my grandma that I am now Thumbelina, that I will never be Louise again. But when I told her, I don't think it sunk in. She just kept smiling and singing some dumb Beatles song. My grandma and grandpa love the Beatles and they're always dancing around the living room to "I Want to Hold Your Hand."

I'm standing at this table, looking around for penguin salt shakers, but I don't see anything like that. Then I notice this humongous cupboard with a long mirror down the front. I'm looking at myself in the mirror and wondering if there is any way Benny McCartney would think I am in ninth grade, even though I'm in seventh grade and have the unfortunate appearance of a fourth grader. I look down at my body and whisper, "Grow, you stupid idiot."

As I am standing there, the man selling the cupboard shows me a little secret drawer. "See this?" he says. "People used to hide their diaries in here. It's a great place for something like that." I am thinking this might be the perfect thing for me. When you have a grandpa like I do, you need a cupboard like this.

Next thing you know, something really hazy crazy happens. As my grandma says, "Life is full to the brim with the mysterious and the amazing." That is her answer for almost everything. I used to think it was a very ho-hum thing to say. But now I'm reconsidering because suddenly Benny McCartney walks by. I'm not kidding you. He walks past me. I see his face and for a moment I feel like a mini tornado just ripped through me, and it isn't a pleasant little tornado. It's dark, and signposts are spinning around. Everything's blurry. I feel like somebody punched me in the stomach. Benny's carrying a big box and he doesn't see me. I back away and I feel like I'm trying to move in a pool of deep water. I feel so dizzy I might fall to the ground. I can see he has a book in his pocket and I can see the title. It seems to be called *On the Road* by Jack Kerouac.

Before I know it, he's gone. Boom. And I need to talk to Reni. Am I supposed to be feeling like I can't breathe? This doesn't feel like a crush. With Frosty the Snowman, I used to get this secret happy feeling. It was with me all through first grade. But Reni says that crush doesn't count because he melted into thin air in the end and also because what idiot would fall in love with a snowman?

I take a deep breath and go back to my grandma and grandpa. They are poking through old dingy boxes of bottles in someone's booth. My grandpa stands up, looking all dented and disappointed. He brushes the dust off his knees sadly and offers Grandma a hand.

Then I show them the cupboard I have decided I want, with the cool secret drawer in the back. Grandma and Grandpa look kind of overwhelmed and quite small standing before it. And my grandma says, "Oh, honey, of course. Honey. Honey. Honey. Of course."

Then she and Grandpa stare at the cupboard like two wistful mice looking up at a giant they have to slay.

Grandpa goes off to pay for the cupboard and to arrange for someone to deliver it to the condo. I leave the building, looking down at the stupid bloodred stamp on my hand that says SOUTH POTTSBORO ANTIQUE SHOW. I can't wait to wash it off. My grandma is back at the car with a bag of antique lace she just bought and I lean against the car door in a wish-I-was-on-the-moon sort of way.

I look at my grandma. Behind her head the sky is an icy, crystal, pure winter blue. I want to ask her why she acted weird when Benny McCartney delivered the pizza that night. I'm just about to form the words when suddenly this memory pops up in front of me, like someone just shook one of those paperweights full of snow and when the snow settles in there you see the scene clearly. *I'm in the side yard at my house on Cinnamon Street. I'm running. The grass is bright green. I'm falling toward it. I need to get to the front yard without throwing up or fainting. I have to get there. I have to, have to, have to get there before I fall over.*

"Honey?" says my grandma. "Are you okay?" She looks at me for a minute and then her face splinters and shatters and she puts her arms around me and gives me one of her squeeze-you-to-death-forget-about-breathing grandma hugs.

Chapter Five

I can't believe I'm at school down in the basement in Merit Madson country. The halls in this part of the school smell wet and like chlorine because of the swimming pool nearby. There's a watery echo in the air, and everybody who brushes by me has wet hair tucked back behind their ears in a busy, belonging kind of way that makes me feel like somebody just clicked the UN-FRIEND button when they got to my name.

When I was at North last year, I used to come over here for gymnastic meets. Then these halls were dark and gloomy because we were just the visiting team and we didn't know anything about the school. I guess I still feel like a visiting team. Like no matter how many freaking showers I take, I can never wash away that feeling of being a visiting team. Even though this is my school now. Even though I quit gymnastics.

The only reason I'm down here today in these halls is because I left a brand-new leotard behind in my old locker in the gymnastics room. I stop now in front of Coach Tull's office and practice room. There's this little window high in the door and because I'm small, I have to get on my tiptoes to see in.

Up on my toes, I can see the whole flipping gymnastics team sitting in a circle in there surrounded by the equipment. Coach is talking about "inner poise" and the importance of stretching. Blah. Blah. Blah. I can see Merit Madson and Janie Brevette. They stand out like somebody took a yellow Day-Glo marker and drew a big circle around them. Merit is leaning against the pommel horse with one arm over it in a very loving way, like it's her personal pet, even though we never use those pommel horses.

Suddenly this seventh grader named Sue McCaleb appears next to me, like out of freaking nowhere. She looks down at me like I'm from Loserland, USA. I have to look *up* at her and this fries me big-time because she can peek in the window with ease while I'm hopping around next to her like a dorky M&M on springs. "Are they starting earlier now? I've been in another section," she goes. "Are we late?"

"I wouldn't know. I'm not on the team anymore. I had to quit because of schoolwork," I say.

"Oh," she says, "I didn't know that, Louise." And then she looks away, like I just died or something. "Well, you gotta do what you gotta do. Right?" she says, winking at me. I hate when kids your own age wink at you. Then she opens the door and sweeps into the circle on the floor in the practice room. For a moment the door stands open and Merit Madson spots me. Her pointed-arrow eyes go shooting through me. Janie starts smirking. All the while I just stand there in the door like I'm frozen, like my feet are iced up and stuck to the floor, like I just landed on planet Jupiter and somehow I forgot my space suit.

Then the lunch bell rings and I am spared. I break away and start running down the hall. When I get through the maze of tunnels and staircases and swarms of kids, I push into the cafeteria. I don't know anybody who has first-period lunch and I hate trying to find somewhere to sit. I always feel like a lost airplane circling the crowds, trying to find a friendly runway where I can land.

Even though he's in seventh grade at North, sometimes Henderson is over at South for lunch, which today could be helpful. How this kid ended up as a messenger for the assistant principal here at South, I do not know. This gives him "mobility," he says, which means he can leave his school at any given moment and show up unexpectedly at South. He carries this leather messenger pouch with kids' exams and detention notices, and sometimes you see him coming out of some room, usually the cafeteria.

Ah, now I see Henderson. He's sitting at a table

having a big hot lunch. He's got a gigantic plate of pasta in front of him. Henderson is the kind of kid who doesn't mind sitting alone. He doesn't see it as an announcement of his loserhood.

"Thumb!" he says, looking up. This kid never calls me Louise, which I appreciate. Henderson, on the other hand, really likes his name. He thinks it sounds like a cool butler's name in an old-fashioned movie, like "Bring up the car, Henderson." Or "That will be all, Henderson."

"Hey, Hen," I go, sitting down next to him. "What's in the pouch? Somebody's No Child Left Behind exam?"

"Very funny," says Henderson. "I'm not at liberty to divulge the assistant principal's private papers." He takes the leather pouch and hugs it against him. His long plaid flannel arms wrap around it. Then he slips it under his chair. "Top secret," he says. "And I'm starving. Wanna bite?"

"Henderson, you're always starving," I say.

"Hey, this is a special day," he says. "I lucked out as soon as I walked in the front door here. I meet this kid who's being wheeled off in agony to have a possible appendix operation. He gives me his meal ticket for the day. I kid you not. There's a sandwich in my backpack you can have if you want."

"I'm not hungry," I say. "I'm in mourning over a leotard."

"It's a special day for other special reasons," Henderson says, smiling. It's an inner smile that glows, like there's this cool private party going on inside Henderson.

"Like what?" I say.

"Like I finished another chapter in my space murder mystery. Now the robots from Mars are aggressive. And the robots from Venus are passive-aggressive."

"Ha ha, like my grandpa," I say. "My grandma always calls him passive-aggressive when he won't take out the garbage. Wanna read me the new parts now or later? And where's this sandwich?"

Henderson tosses me his backpack, and I go looking for the sandwich. I pass a pair of binoculars. About five candy bars. Some night-sky books. Henderson uses the binoculars to watch birds, especially pigeons. Everybody in North and South Pottsboro hates pigeons. But Henderson loves them.

I find the sandwich in waxed paper. It's got lettuce and cheese and olives and pickles and everything else in the world on it. Henderson is one of these people who can eat and eat and still be hungry and skinny, which is why his dad calls him "the garbage disposal."

Now Henderson gets out his novel. He spreads his papers and outlines all over the table. In most of his chapters somebody gets shot and bleeds all over the place. It's awesome. Even though it's noisy here, Henderson reads me his new chapter of *The Space Walk Murders*. After he's done, I say, "Wow, Henderson, you've really written forty-five pages?"

And he goes, "Forty-eight pages now." And we both sit there in awe of all those pages and all the terrible things that happened to the robots and the astronauts.

I have my books for my afternoon classes on the table and Henderson picks up the one on top and starts leafing through it. The pages fall open right away to the place where I tucked the note from the pizza stalker. Every time I see that note my heart does a string of mini flips.

"So," says Hen, reaching for the note, "here it is."

"Yup," I say. "You're the expert analyzer. What do you think?"

"Hmm," says Henderson, cleaning his glasses with a napkin. Then he puts his glasses back on, looks at the note, holds it closer, and soon he goes in his backpack and gets out a magnifying glass. I'm sitting here waiting like a patient in a doctor's office while Henderson studies the note under the lens and jots down a long list in his notebook. Then he looks up. "This kid is a righty, not a lefty. You can tell by the slant of the sentence."

"A righty?" I say.

"Yep," goes Henderson. "Twenty percent of the population are lefties. So we just reduced our search among the possibilities by twenty percent."

"Oh, okay," I say. "Anything else?"

"I'll have to take this home for further analysis," he says. He puts the note in his pocket.

"Hey, take good care of it and give it back soon," I say. "It's probably the only one I'll ever get."

"Okay, Thumb, I'll do some tests and get back to you with answers soon."

Henderson rolls up his novel and stuffs it in his backpack. Then he says, "See that kid over there? He actually pushed me when I walked by him today. My pasta almost slipped into a side pouch of his backpack. I don't even go to this school. I don't even know this kid. Therefore, I have to assume he's a true ork."

"What's an ork?" I say.

"Ork is two notches worse than dork," says Henderson.

"Oh," I say.

"But I overlooked it this time."

"Because he's on the wrestling team?" I say.

"Well, because today is a special day and I didn't want to ruin it with a broken back," he says.

"Oh, but Reni and I would have visited you in the hospital," I say. "Reni would have drawn smiley faces all over your body cast."

"Sweet," says Henderson, reaching again into his backpack.

"So why's today so special?" I say.

"Well, it's special because a while ago, this gorgeous tiny meteorite fell from the sky in faraway Iowa," says

Henderson, beaming. "This little meteorite could be a piece of the moon or a chunk of Mars or part of a comet. Writers would call it a falling star. And by chance it got put up for sale on eBay. I kid you not. And I was the high bidder last week. I bought it for fifteen dollars."

"Cool," I say.

"And it arrived in the mail today. A real piece of the universe from far, far away. It came to me, Henderson Elliot, 14 Nutmeg Street, North Pottsboro, Mass. After all those millions of years of travel through unknown space, a falling star ends up here." He opens his fingers and there is a little, shiny, gold-flecked rock lying in the center of Henderson's palm.

Chapter Six

I'm just getting home from school, thinking about how my grandma says I used to be "very poetic." Sunsets used to be my all-time favorite. Now I hate them. I used to get all high scores in the artistic part of the gymnastic routine. Now I hate gymnastics. Everything was different before, when I lived on Cinnamon Street.

I'm just going up the steps to our condo. Suddenly I stop. Boom. I can't believe this. Someone has drawn a big heart in pink chalk on the cement porch in front of our door. A heart? What?

I step back, turn my head away, and then I look again just to make sure it's really there. It is. Well, it could just be that some kids were playing out here, making hopscotch boards. In the snow? I look around. I don't see any sign of any kids. I step right in the middle of the heart, my snowy boots making footprints all over it. My own heart does a couple more flips. The pizza stalker strikes again.

I don't know anything about Benny McCartney. I think I have to take matters into my own hands. I *have* to get to know him better, even though he makes me dizzy and wobbly when I see him. I have to trust Reni in the crush department because Reni wrote the book on crushes, at least the one called *Crushing Justin Bieber: Ten Ways to Cry Your Heart Out.*

When I get upstairs, I go in my room and shut the door. My grandparents always look so hurt when I go in my room, like why didn't I want to sit on the couch with them and discuss our rising condo fees? I decide to get out my cell and call Reni. "Reni," I say.

"Hey ho," she goes. (All the Elliots say hey ho instead of hi. It's an Elliot family trait.)

"Reni, hi. Help!" I say. Reni is the kind of friend you can count on. I mean ever since I spotted for her in gymnastics class and she fell off the balance beam and I caught her, we've been cool. Well, I didn't exactly catch her. She landed on me. "Reni, somebody drew a heart on the outside porch of our condo building."

"Wow. This is getting intense. You weren't imagining it, were you? I mean maybe you're just seeing hearts cause you're crushing Benny."

"No, this was an obvious heart. An intentional heart. I think."

"I have an idea. Listen to me. Order another pizza. Then you can see Benny again."

"Do I want to see him again?" I say.

"Of course you do. How many letters like this do you think you're going to get in your life? How many hearts are you going to find on your doorstep?"

"Oh," I say. "Okay, I'll order another pizza, but I might not get Benny. Sometimes I get this kid from South who carries the pizza on its side so all the mushrooms end up huddled in the corner. I think his name is Newton Mancini. If my parents named me Newton, I'd apply for new parents. Is that possible?"

"I doubt it," says Reni. "You'd have kids applying all over the place."

"True," I say. "Reni, can I come over? I need more consultation in the crush department. I mean, I'm lost here."

"Yeah, but we can't disturb my sister. She has a poetry slam and an art show coming up at the Chaff and Plow Café in a month."

"No problem, Reni. I'll ask my grandma to drop me off, okay?"

"Okay," says Reni, "but we have to be quiet. Annais is sooo creative."

My grandma puts on her long brown vintage coat with the fake leopard collar. She loves vintage clothes. "How does it look?" she says, turning toward Grandpa.

"Should have bought the hat, beautiful," he says.

Grandma smiles back at me. "Good thing he's part blind," she says. "Get your satchel."

"What's a satchel?" I say. "You mean my backpack, Grandma? What for?"

"Aren't you studying over there?"

"No, Grandma, Reni and I aren't even in the same school. Um, well, her brother, Henderson, um, wants to read us a few pages of his outer space murder mystery. He's applying to some writing camp. *That's* why I'm going over there."

"Ah, Henderson," says Grandpa. "Every time I hear that name, I always wonder whatever happened to all the old regular names like Tom and Jack and Harry and Bob. I guess the Bill Smiths of the world are an extinct species these days." Grandpa looks kind of sad and he puts on his dorky plaid wool cap that looks like some dog took it and ran with it around the block five times, dropped it in a puddle, and then brought it back to Grandpa.

"You can stay here, honey bear. I'll buzz her over," says my grandma, and then Grandma and Grandpa get all smoochy like she's going away for some extended trip to Europe or something.

We pull up in front of the Elliots' house on Nutmeg Street. The streets in North Pottsboro are all named after spices. My mom and dad and me used to live on Cinnamon Street. It's three streets over from Nutmeg. I think Coriander and Paprika are in between. I mean, how cool is North Pottsboro? I mean, it makes South Pottsboro look like a dump, which it is.

I hear someone coming to the door when I push the bell. My grandma is waiting in the car, all nervous that nobody's home. "Darling," she calls from the car window, "ring the bell."

"Duh, Grandma," I'm thinking. She keeps waving good-bye from the car and then she beeps the horn and it's so loud, I'm ready to crawl under the Elliots' porch and die.

Reni opens the door and she's all bubbly and happy to see me. She looks at me, checking for outward signs of a crush, and then she nods her head in a knowing Reni way. I walk in the door, and Reni's mom is in the living room watching a DVD and stirring a bowl of cake batter at the same time.

The Elliots are an awesome family. There are three kids plus a mom and a dad, and it looks to me like everybody's entire wardrobe is strewn around the living room. There are sweaters, shirts, shoes, and jeans all over the floor. Reni's mom has on a pair of slippers with big teddy bears on the front.

"Hi, Louise," says Reni's mom, and those words have such a nice warm ring to them (even though she's got my name all wrong). She doesn't even turn her head to see it's me. She *knows* it's me, like it's as natural as breathing that I'm at the door, like I'm just part of the family. Reni's mom is all bubbly too by nature. The Elliots are just a big bubbly family. I love love love love Reni's mom.

I walk into the living room with Reni, and I stand there. Reni's mom gets up and heads toward the kitchen, still holding her big mixing bowl. I open my arms and she puts down the bowl and gives me a hug. "Mrs. Elliot, adopt me, please," I say looking up at her and putting my hands together like I'm praying.

And she goes, "Okay, you're adopted."

And I go, "Seriously."

Mrs. Elliot has been baking in the kitchen. When she hugs you, you feel like a double vanilla carrot cake just wrapped its arms around you. She goes on to the kitchen, saying, "You're not staying too long, are you? I want Reni to help Annais with her laundry in a little while. Okay, Louise?"

"She's not Louise anymore. Her name is Thumbelina," says Reni. Then she throws her arms around me too and says, "Isn't it cool? It's like a fairy tale. Cause she's small, Mom, get it?"

"What about that room down in the basement?" I whisper to Reni. "Did you ask your mom and dad if I can move in there? I'd fix it up and make it pretty and everything."

"I didn't ask yet," says Reni. She leads me up the soft carpeted stairs. The banister is definitely a part-time coatrack and closet, and on every step, I find somebody's stray shoe.

Mrs. Elliot comes to the bottom of the stairs. "Don't bother your sister. She's painting. Her show at Chaff and Plow Café is next month. Coming to the opening, Louise?" Reni's mom says.

"Of course, Mrs. Elliot, I'll be there. I can't wait. I mean, I'm part of the family, right?" I say.

The carpet is soft and warm on the stairs and everybody in Reni's family is soft and warm. Even Henderson, except he's not chubby, he's tall; and right now he's on his computer in his room, but I see he just got a buzz cut and his ears seem bigger than usual. He looks pink and new, like somebody just threw a bucket of water over him. "They mangled him up at Cutting Edge today," says Reni. "Next time you see Henderson, he'll be wearing a baseball cap."

"Ha ha," I go.

"Henderson," Mrs. Elliot calls, taking a few steps up the stairs. "Can you please explain what happened to all my striped purple tulips in the sunroom? They just started blooming and somebody has cut them all and taken them away. Do you know anything about this?"

Henderson comes out into the hall, holding a big book over his head. "Hey, Thumb," he mumbles through the pages. Then he shouts down the stairs, "What? Why do you always ask me this stuff? Like whenever something happens, it's always me. I've been on my computer all day. I thought I saw Mrs. Barker out the window after she was here for coffee. She was dashing away with a bunch of tulips under her coat."

"Ha ha," Reni says and puts her hands on her hips and frowns at Henderson. Then she pulls me down the hall and whispers, "He's a spy. I know it. He's a thirteen-year-old spy. He's got this camera and he doesn't show anybody what he's photographing and stuff keeps disappearing around here. He's part of the CIA. I know it."

"Is that possible?" I whisper back. "Do they hire kids?"

We pass Annais's room. She's in there painting. She's got a Diana Krall disc going, playing the song "Peel Me a Grape." Reni's older sister is in ninth grade and she's considered the most talented girl at North. Everyone just loves her paintings and her poems. Her mom says, "Annais is ten years ahead of her times and that's being conservative!"

"Everybody calls Annais chubby-beautiful," says Reni. "How come guys love her and she's overweight like me?"

"Maybe it's because Annais acts pretty," I say.

"How do you act pretty?" says Reni.

Finally we get to Reni's room. There's a pink bedspread on her bed and a light with a pink lampshade on the table. Reni collects everything pink. I used to collect penguins. I once had a penguin wristwatch and penguin sunglasses. I throw myself down on her soft rug and look up at her ceiling. She has a poster of Justin Bieber pinned up there. This is a very cool idea.

"Reni," I go.

She goes, "Yeah?"

"Do I really look like I'm crushing somebody? I mean, can you really tell from the outside?"

"Yeah," goes Reni, "of course you can tell. You're, like, all pale and weird-looking. I think we should try to get ahold of some of Benny's notebooks to see if he's writing your name in the margins."

"No, Reni. This doesn't feel right. This is something different. It can't be a crush. And how would we find any notebook of his anyway?" I say.

"Well, Benny probably lives around here. Everybody lives near here," Reni says. "We can take a walk and maybe if we see him you'll be able to tell how you feel."

I sit up and wrap my arms around my legs. I put myself in a little ball. I need to do some flips. Fifty flips would straighten everything out. Followed by a bunch of fast aerial cartwheels and a string of handsprings. Henderson walks by the room outside, still with the book over his head. He stops in the doorway. Reni points to me and says, "A basket case."

Henderson peers out at me from under some pages. I feel like a specimen in a zoo.

"What kind of a basket?" says Henderson. "Indian sweetgrass or pine needle?"

"Ha ha and good-bye, Henderson," says Reni. Then she slams the door and flops down on the rug and stares up at the ceiling. "You know what? Loving Justin Bieber is a one-way street," she says. "I do all the giving and get nothing in return, not even a form letter. *You*, on the other hand, have a handwritten, handmade, one-of-a-kind real letter. The only thing wrong with your situation is *you*. You're on the fence. You're waffling."

"I'm not really on the fence," I say. "I like Benny, I think. I mean, maybe a lot, for all I know. It just doesn't *feel* like it, that's all."

Reni hops up suddenly like a big happy exclamation point. "Of course you do! Let's go ask Annais where this poor adorable lovesick boy lives," she says, looking sweetly, joyously at me. Then she starts jumping up and down and squealing. The Elliots all jump up and down and squeal a lot. Except Henderson. He frowns when they squeal. But he also smiles and laughs when he's sleeping. Reni told me, when they used to share a room, she had to throw stuff at him in the night to keep his laughter level down.

Reni bops into Annais's room and I follow her. "Guess what," she says with a smile as big and wide as the South Pottsboro I-95 bridge. "*She* got a love letter."

"No way," goes Annais, giving a corner of her painting a scrub with a sloppy-looking paintbrush. "From who?"

"It's so cool," says Reni, still bouncing up and down. She's so happy, she reminds me of a second grader on her way to a sleepover. "It's from Benny McCartney. You know? We think he might be lovesick slash embarrassed slash desperate. She hasn't seen him recently. He may be in hiding. If he doesn't show up at school, we'll know he's hurting because she hasn't responded."

Annais's face begins to match the color on the end of her paintbrush, a dark boiling red. "No, Reni. You are an inexperienced dope. He's an older guy. He's in ninth grade. Are you kidding me? You're encouraging Louise to stalk him. Stalkers get in trouble, big-time."

"Thumbelina is her name. If you call her Louise, she's not going to answer you. Right, Thumbelina?"

"This is the real world, girls," says Annais, "and it sounds to me like you're both a couple of potential stalkers."

"Do you think I'm stalking Justin Bieber?" says Reni, rolling her eyes up toward her eyebrows, as if there might be an answer to that question sitting up there.

"No, Reni, how can you stalk someone when you don't even know where they live?" I say.

"Exactly," says Reni. "She's not stalking Benny, because we don't know where he lives. Do you know where he lives, Annais?"

"Look, girls, I need to paint," Annais says, stepping

back with one hand on her hip, looking at her crazy messed-up canvas from a distance. She's wearing a cool painting smock with all these artsy paint splashes all over it. "I bet you two think the center of a painting is important. Right?" says Annais.

"Yeah," Reni and I say in unison.

"Well, to me, all that matters are the edges. I'm working on the textural variations of color along the edges," she says.

Reni and I look at each other. Then I put my hand up over my mouth to squeeze back a major laugh.

"Thumbelina isn't feeling well," says Reni, pushing me out of the room like I'm a loaded laundry cart. "And that's because we have every reason to believe she's in love."

After looking in the phone book, Reni and I set out to walk by a couple of McCartney residences in the area. Paul McCartney of my grandpa's favorite group, the Beatles, isn't the only McCartney in the world. There are at least four others in North Pottsboro. But tell that to my grandpa. My grandpa says he's the most ferocious, dedicated Beatle fan out there. To me, that means fifty years of listening to the same songs over and over again.

It's snowing again. My feet are freezing. I'm thinking about that woman mountain climber Henderson told me about. Why didn't anyone hike down the cliff and look in all the ice crevasses for her? Why did they let her fall off the mountain and freeze to death? I need to ask Henderson. But I couldn't today because when someone has an open book covering his head, it's hard to strike up a conversation.

Reni and I are walking down Nutmeg Street and crossing over to Coriander. Snow is dancing around us, and Reni just keeps trudging along. I'm not sure where we're going, but we're making a little path in the lost whiteness all around us. Our voices are puffy and muffled in the quiet snow falling. This is my old neighborhood. I used to be "a Cinnamon Street kid." I had billions of blue ribbons and white ribbons for tumbling, for cartwheels, for walkovers. . . . I was a daddy and mommy's girl. I had a daddy and a mommy. We had a house with two porches. Kids used to come over after school. I used to be a normal size too. I wasn't little. I was average. I liked being average. It was fun being everyday and ho-hum and just like everybody else. That was before everybody started growing and I stopped.

Reni gets ahead of me and soon she becomes a bright blur in the soft, falling heavy whiteness everywhere. "Come on," she calls, "I think he lives on Coriander Street. This way."

The houses are covered in snow and have pointed roofs and chimneys puffing and little winding paths like in a fairy tale. We get on Cinnamon Street and we pass number 14. It's a green house. "Reni," I call out. "There's my old house."

I stop in the snow and stand there and look at the house. It's unoccupied. Empty. I feel its emptiness in my stomach.

"This is where you used to live?" Reni says, puffing back through the snow toward me. Her cheeks are Reni red and her Reni round face is full of light.

"That's a cool little house. I didn't know this was your house."

"Yup," I say.

The tree is still in the backyard. I can see its sprawling arms, its twisted branches. It's all knotted and gnarled just by the back door. I guess I once climbed that tree and wouldn't come down for five hours. My grandpa had to get up there and pull me out of it. They said I was screaming. You'd think I'd remember something so weird as that. But no. My grandma says I have blocked a whole week out of my conscious mind. She says I have forgotten everything that happened. She says I'm protecting myself. But how could I do that when I don't even know what a conscious mind is?

Reni and I sit on the snowy front steps of number 14 Cinnamon Street. We don't say anything much. If Reni were to ask me what happened here, I wouldn't tell her. I would run away and never speak to her again, if I could remember. But I can't remember. Reni might even know what happened, but she doesn't talk about it.

"You had a lot of friends then," she says.

"Yup," I say.

"You don't want to talk to them anymore."

"Nope," I say.

"You were so so good at gymnastics."

"Yup," I say again. And then I don't feel anything except the soft snowflakes landing lightly on my frozen face.

Chapter Seven

Someone is outside cleaning the sidewalk below our condo right now with a very noisy snow blower. It sounds like our building is being dive-bombed.

"For goodness' sakes," goes my grandma, "why don't they just use a shovel to clear the sidewalk? That noisy thing is doing nothing but blowing snow around and polluting our ears. Men," she says, frowning at Grandpa.

"Well," says Grandpa, "when I invented that machine, I should have made it quieter. Same thing with the wheel. I should have made it rounder, right, pal?"

"Ha ha, Grandpa," I say.

"Ready to go?" says Grandpa, doing a few dumb Tai Chi moves and then grabbing my nose and pretending to steal it, like I'm a first grader or something. I don't laugh and I'm not going to act like a little kid, even though I may look like one.

Then my cell rings and I open it. Whenever Henderson calls, his photo pops up showing him wearing a cardboard spray-painted space suit, his costume for a party last year at Halloween.

"Hey, Thumb," he says.

"Hey, Hen," I say. "What's up?"

"Well," he goes, "this is breaking news. This is confidential. This is top secret data."

"What?" I say.

"Working at the library here, reading, I've discovered that dinosaurs never disappeared at all," he whispers.

"They didn't?" I say.

"No, they didn't and you're not to tell the Dinosaur Research and Development Foundation if they call, okay?"

"Okay," I say. "And I was just about to give them a buzz."

"Well, don't bother," he says. "This is top secret. Listen. You can hear some dinosaurs outside right now singing in the snowy trees."

"What?" I go.

"They're birds. Birds. They became smaller and smaller over millions of years. Dinosaurs evolved into birds."

"Cool," I say. "But we don't have any trees or birds over here in South Pottsboro anyway. I haven't seen a bird in years. Ha ha."

"Ho ho," says Henderson. "By the way, as I was leaving school today, no joke, this kid in my English class out of the blue gives me a gift certificate to Starbucks for two mocha Frappuccinos and two stale cookies. And I don't even know the kid. That's the way things have been going in my life since I bought that meteorite on eBay. So we can have a tall Frappuccino tomorrow afternoon, thanks to a beautiful little falling star, and I can read you another new chapter."

"Oh, okay," I say.

"Oops, gotta go, Thumb. They're closing the library. Hey, wait! Excuse me. I'm still here," he calls out. "Wait, come back." I hear pounding on a door. Then Henderson clicks off and his photo disappears.

Henderson is always getting shut up in that library. Once he had to stay all night locked up in there. He slept in the rowboat full of pillows in the children's reading room. But he blogged about it later and got a lot of comments. (Reni says he planned the whole thing.)

About this dinosaur stuff. Henderson always has all kinds of facts and all kinds of nonfacts. I mean, if you want to know the population of Pokeweed, Pennsylvania, Henderson knows, which is sometimes cool and sometimes like, "Uh, did you just get off the train from Dorkville, USA?"

Just now my grandma is saying, "Henderson is cute, but immature. Boys are always a little behind girls until later. Right, Grandpa?"

"I was way cool," says Grandpa. "I was never immature."

"Oh, right," says Grandma, crossing her arms and smiling. She and Grandpa are planning to go out for sushi tonight, so they're both all cheerful. Grandpa and

Grandma get all excited about any kind of dinner on the horizon. When they go out, they always drink French wine and they go on and on about the woody barrel flavors and the overtones of boring fruity peelings. Meanwhile they're both getting red in the face and rowdy in a senior kind of way.

Grandpa wants to make reservations at the sushi restaurant, but before he does, he wants to know what the restaurant looks like. He wants to check it out in person. It's a new place that just opened up in, you guessed it, North Pottsboro.

Because I have no conflicting appointments (how unusual), I accept their invitation to go along. As we walk in the mall entrance, Grandma and Grandpa are holding hands again and I'm pretending to whistle and look at the floor. Being small and short, I usually see a lot of the floor anyway. I'm always the first to spot knotholes, nicked nails, and stuck bubble gum. A valuable asset. Ha ha.

Then suddenly we pass by my dream store. It's called My Princess Prom and this store was created just for me. Whoever made this store *knew* me and knew I would die and go to heaven every time I walk in there. If Reni and I were billionaires, we would buy every single dress they have.

But the problem is not the dress. The problem is the guy. Which brings me back to *the letter* and the pink chalk heart on my doorstep. I mean, I have to admit I do have a tingly hopeful feeling because of this. I wouldn't describe it as happy because, since last year and what happened, that word is not part of my daily vocab. I guess the best word to describe all this is *confused*.

"Louise," goes my grandma. She smiles and spins around as we stop in front of My Princess Prom. "Louise, wouldn't it be fun to go in there? You could try on some dresses. We could buy you one. What do you say, Grandpa?" Sometimes when my grandma talks to my grandpa, her voice goes up a notch higher than usual and she tries to look all cute and helpless around him. And my dumb grandpa falls for the act every time.

I smile at the store and nod at my grandma and grandpa in a very approving way. So we walk in the door of My Princess Prom. Then my cell phone rings. I look at my grandma and she shrugs her shoulders, so I answer it. "Hey ho, Reni," I say.

And Reni goes, "You are never gonna believe this. I was in the school library earlier and guess who I saw?"

"Who?" I say.

"Who do you think? Benny McCartney! He was sitting there so sweetly filling out a form, and guess which hand he was writing with?"

"His left hand?" I say.

"No, his right hand," says Reni. "Benny's a righty! He's a righty."

"Oh no, I can't believe this," I say. "I have to sit down. I feel dizzy. I'm at My Princess Prom with my grandparents. They're gonna buy me a dress."

"Perfect," says Reni. "Couldn't be better. You're going to need that dress. Buy it for Benny. He's going to love it."

"Fine," I say. "Okay. I think."

When we get off the phone I look up and the dresses seem to swirl around me, ribbons and lace and silky flowers. My mom used to like to wear pretty fluffy dresses. Blue was her favorite color. Not a dark blue but a pale blue. An eggshell blue, faint and breakable like a morning sky.

I believe I have already mentioned that I am, uh, immature-looking for my age? I am thirteen, but I usually have to look in the children's department for clothes. Kids who are big want to be small, and kids who are small want to be big. Trust me. I know. I'm small and I hate it. Because teachers think I'm in fourth grade and guys look right over my head, thinking I'm somebody's twerp little sister. The fact that Reni is very big and I am very small causes her dad to call us Abbott and Costello, these two stupid not-funny comedians from a hundred years ago. Ha ha.

I guess I should have stayed on the gymnastics team because there my small size is what my grandma calls "an asset." She goes, "Oh, we all have to learn to use our 'assets.' The fact that I'm seventy-two is an asset when I'm looking to teach seniors. See what I mean?" But since I'm not on the team anymore, I have no need to be small. So I want to grow. Now.

They have all these gorgeous dresses arranged by color. Which one would Thumbelina have worn when she sat in the center of a delicate flower with her beautiful prince, getting married finally after suffering great hardships living with a bunch of weird animals who didn't get her? I mean, if a big ugly mole came up and asked me to marry him, I would pass out cold and have to be taken to the ER in North Pottsboro. Pronto. To be quite honest, I do NOT want to die in South Pottsboro.

Maybe I should get a dress to match Benny McCartney's eyes. I think Reni would approve of that. I mean, he wouldn't have to know why I was wearing it. No pressure or anything like that. But I'm not even sure what color his eyes are.

"Look, honey," says Grandma, "isn't this one a dream?" She pulls out a net-covered light green silk dress with a matching crown of flowers. Grandpa is smiling. He has what my English teacher calls an "amused smile" on his face.

"Ah, maybe he doesn't hate being retired after all," Grandma says, putting her arm around me and looking up at Grandpa. I'm not listening. I hold the flower crown in my hands. It's so perfect! Nobody could call me Abbott and Costello if I had *that* on my head.

"Oh, I love this dress," I say. "Do you think you have one in my size?"

The girl selling the clothes is probably three years older than me but she thinks I'm just some little kid.

It's totally annoying. She has this look on her face, a frown covered up with a smirk, covered up with a smile.

"Well, we do have a few *very* small sizes on this rack," the salesgirl says. Grandpa smiles at her like she's so cute and sweet and so adorable. I hate Grandpa. I'm never speaking to him again.

"Here's the same dress," says Grandma, "in a size one. We are very lucky to find this." She winks at the salesgirl. While I go into the dressing room with the to-die-for pale green dress, Grandma and Grandpa get all cozy chatting away with the stuck-up snotty salesgirl. Grandma is out there talking about my size issues. It's like she's telling that girl my deepest, darkest secrets and fears. Then Grandma ups and says, "Well, she hasn't developed fully yet, and finding clothes in her size can be challenging." It is the "fully developed" part that I am dying over. Thanks a lot, Grandma.

I try the dress on and it fits me perfectly. I look in the mirror and it seems like I was born to wear this dress. Like I'm meant to wear it. Once you have found your inner fairy tale, you can't help but act it out! Don't laugh, Merit Madson. I turn in a circle alone in the dressing room.

My grandma and grandpa end up buying me the dress with the green silk underskirt and the net overlay and, best of all, the crown of rosebuds and violets. When we get home, I hang it up on a hook on the wall right opposite the couch. That's the place where most normal people have a good cable TV with maybe a 36 x 48 inch screen that gets 120 channels, but where we have nothing but a blank wall. My grandma does not like large television sets or cable TV.

Grandma and Grandpa are ready to go out to the sushi restaurant. Grandma has on one of her 1950s vintage dresses. "Doesn't this look like the dresses we saw today?" she says. "Things just come back around, don't they? Honey, we'll see you in a couple of hours. Be positive."

They leave, waving and shutting the door behind them, and suddenly a kind of snowy sunset loneliness settles in around me. I'm flopped on the organic couch with my stupid child's-size-12 feet on the coffee table. I'm sitting here being positive, staring at the light moss green Thumbelina dress that is hanging before me on the wall like an impossible dream.

Chapter Eight

It's nearing the end of March, and we've had more snow. Record snowfall this year. Anything living seems to be buried under an avalanche. Reni and I have made no progress with the pizza stalker. I haven't seen Benny anywhere. It has crossed my mind that Newton Mancini may have left me the note. He had delivered the pizza the night before and it's possible we didn't see the note that night. I'm thinking, what do I know about Newton? Well, my grandma is friends with his mom and she says Newton has diabetes. And I know they call him the Valentine Man at school because on Valentine's Day, every girl at South gets a valentine card in her locker from Newton. Even the teachers and the librarians and the secretaries. So this could very well be Newton.

This afternoon my grandma is watching that movie *Thelma and Louise* again. My grandma and grandpa watch that movie a lot. It was my mom's favorite movie. I think she named me Louise because of it. It's a really dumb movie because in the end Thelma and Louise drive off a cliff and die. Always at the end, Grandma and Grandpa press their heads together and they both start in with the big crying festival.

Today when the phone rings, Grandma stops the video, and Thelma's face is caught in a strange blur just at the edge of the cliff before they drive off it.

I pick up the phone. It's on a small table next to the couch. "Hello," I say.

"Hello, Louise, it's your dad. How are you doing, sweetheart? Miss you."

"Fine," I say.

"In school? Doing your homework?"

"Yup," I say.

"My stepdaughter, you know her — Dearie — she says seventh grade is a bust. Tough stuff, I guess. Is that right?"

"Yup," I say.

"Well, you hang in there, kiddo. You're gonna knock 'em dead. Okay? Miss you," he says again.

"Okay," I say.

"Hey, is your grandma there? I'd like to talk to her. She needs to put the house on Cinnamon Street up for sale. It shouldn't be sitting there empty. It's up to her. Have you rented it yet? I mean, if you and she don't want the house, you could sell it to me. I'd be glad to buy it. I want to be the *first* person to know. Okay? After I buy it, I'll get it rented that very day. We should take care of this, honey. Like grown-ups. Right? So let me speak to your grandma."

"Grandma," I say, "it's my dad. He wants to talk to you."

"I'm about to take a bath, Louise. My bath is ready," my grandma says, and she walks away down the back hall and closes several doors.

"She's taking a bath," I say.

"You tell her to call me. We need to talk. She doesn't call me back, Louise. We need to clear this up. And you're coming to the city to see us sometime soon, sweetheart. Right? We'll pick you up at the airport. Dearie really enjoys your company. Okay?"

"Okay," I say.

"All right, then?" he says. "Okay?"

"Yup," I say.

"We'll talk soon. Okay?"

"Okay," I say and I hang up the phone.

When Grandma comes back in the room, she's got cream on her face and it's thick and white and it looks like a mask. Her hair is pulled back really tightly in a hair clip, like that hair clip is holding all of her together. Like if you took off the hair clip, everything about my grandma would scatter.

She rewinds the video now, the movie of Thelma and Louise. It makes a fast hissing noise. We see Thelma and Louise backing away from the cliff. Away. Away. In superfast motion, they take back everything they did in a frenzy until we get to the beginning again, where Thelma and Louise look like two normal smiling housewives. Now my grandma zips the old-fashioned portable TV back into the suitcase where she keeps it on a shelf. Then we both sit there on the couch, staring at that stupid suitcase. Soon my grandma throws her arms around me and rocks me back and forth, back and forth. I have a feeling the rocking is comforting her, while all it does is make me very very dizzy.

Chapter
Nine

Grandma wants me to take the laundry down to the condo basement. I'm like, "Oh, Grandma, I'm so tired. I got too much sleep last night. Can't Grandpa do it?" Grandma pulls a stuffed canvas bag out into the middle of the kitchen and hands me the pull string like she's offering me some big fat dog on a leash that I have to go walk.

"I'll do it if I can move to Cinnamon Street. Can I?" I say. Grandma closes her eyes and bites her lower lip.

I pull the laundry bag out the door and down the long hall. I'm thinking about that book Benny had in his pocket that day I saw him at the antique show. It was called *On the Road* by Jack somebody or other. I'm thinking to myself, *This is a must-read.*

They have this little condo library downstairs in the basement by the washer and dryer. There's a shelf of paperbacks that people have brought down to share or to donate. I look through them now, hoping to come across Benny's book, but all I find are paperbacks like *The Butcher's Curse* and *The Bloody Grinding Ax* and stuff like that. Judging from their choice of reading material, I'm wondering if all the tenants in this condo are secret psychopaths and repressed killers. Judging from the readers' tastes around here, Henderson may be sitting on a bestseller.

Grandpa is down here in the basement, reading the newspaper. Grandpa just loves this basement. Grandma calls it "his lair." She'll go, "Go get the old fox out of his lair, will you. It's dinnertime."

I'm looking around at all the books on some lower

shelves now. I'm humming and trying to decide whether I should wear my new green net and silk dress to Annais's opening at the Plow and Chaff Café in a few weeks. We need to think of a way to invite Benny to the party. Then, if he's going to be there, wouldn't it be advantageous for me to be wearing a drop-dead-beautiful prom dress? Of course, I will have read the book *On the Road* and I can go, "Oh, you mean Jack Kangaroo? Oh, yeah, I met him last year. He's very cool."

Come to think of it, Henderson has probably read the book and I can ask him what it's about and then I won't even have to read it.

So I call Henderson on my cell, which doesn't always work down here in Lost Laundry Land, but I don't want to go back up to the apartment cause my grandma is flying all over our place today, washing curtains and going at secret corners with her vacuum cleaner. She's got this ancient vacuum cleaner that she's been using for fifty years and it looks like a flipping anteater to me. It's got this long plaid snout and you get the feeling when that thing is on, nothing is sacred or safe from its mighty sucking ability, not even your own thoughts.

I brush away a nice spot for myself and then I boost myself up on the folding table next to the dryer and pick up my cell. The stealthy fox goes past me with his reading glasses perched on his forehead, saying, "Pal, I'm gonna go check the mail and I'll be right back." Grandpa is also wearing an earpiece from his phone in his ear. He wears this black bulky stupid thing constantly, but it is sooo lame because he never gets calls from anyone.

When Henderson picks up, I go, "Hey, Hen, it's me."

And Henderson says, "Thumb!"

"Have you by chance read this book called *On the Road* by Jack Karo-something? Benny McCartney had the book in his pocket and I was wondering what it's about. In case I see Benny, can you give me a quick rundown?"

"I have read it," he says. "My sister Annais adores the book. It's like her bible. You're planning on seeing Benny M?"

"Well, it's a plan that hasn't materialized. Yet," I say.

"Peculiar," goes Henderson, "Strange. Bizarre. Unfathomable. Baffling."

"Blah blah blah," I go. "Why is it Annais's bible?"

"There's this teacher at North who is really into Jack Kerouac. He makes everybody in his class read *On the Road* and memorize pages and pages of it."

"Oh, is Benny in his class?" And then a second later I say, "Is Annais in his class?" Henderson doesn't answer. Then my cell starts beeping and blinking and carrying on like crazy cause the battery is low and it needs to be recharged and then, boom, it dies.

Grandpa shuffles by me, still hopefully wearing his cell phone earpiece. He's carrying a small pile of letters. He sets them on the table next to me and nestles back in his chair and starts reading the newspaper again. So with nothing else to do, I start counting the dust bunnies on the top of the dryer and then I reach for the letters and flip through them. I am sure they will all be for Grandma. She's big-time popular with a huge set of gloomy-looking eighty-year-old granola-crunching wish-I-wuzzers.

On the top of the pile is a letter addressed to me. Me? Louise Terrace. Me. (Yes, that's me. The minute I was born I was given my mom's last name.) I pick up the letter and look at the return address. It says *Coach Jay Tull, South Pottsboro Middle School.* Coach Tull has written me a letter? What?

Immediately, I grab the letter and rip open the envelope. I begin to read a nicely typed formal-looking letter with an official signature at the bottom. It says:

Dear Louise Terrace,

I am writing to you in the hope that you will reconsider your decision to quit the South Pottsboro Girls' Gymnastics Team. This was a great blow to our winning average, and your absence was most heartfully felt. I would recommend you drop by my office to discuss this decision and to talk about the

possibility of your imminent return. My office hours
are posted on my door.

>   *Sincerely yours,*
>   *Coach Jay Tull*

I look over at the space down here where my balance beam used to be. I used to come down here and practice all the time. Now I am thinking about Mrs. Stevenson, who bought that beam at the yard sale. It actually took four very large dorks to carry it away in that snowstorm, it was so heavy. Who were they? Maybe I could track them down and bully them into bringing it back. This letter from Coach Tull is causing me considerable confusion and agony. Perhaps the coach does not understand my situation. If I go back to the team, I can expect to enjoy an extremely short life span. I may not make it out of seventh grade at all, I mean, considering the charm and power and size of Merit Madson.

In my mind I quickly write back a million letters to Coach Tull . . . saying things like *Dear Coach Tull,*

What are you, crazy? Can I count on you to handle my funeral arrangements in the near future?

Why does Merit Madson hate me so much? Obviously because I'm stunted in my growth. I'm immature, undeveloped. Small. Terribly childish-looking. Unable to grow. Over-the-top dorky Thumbelina, princess of the flowers, stuck in the bud stage never to bloom.

Chapter Ten

I decide to Google Benny McCartney and to stop this dopey waffling. A long list comes up on my computer. It seems there's a Benny McCartney with white hair who runs a bank in Omaha, Nebraska. There's another Benny McCartney who's a librarian in Kalamazoo, Michigan, and there's a teenager in Alaska named Benny McCartney who just won a dogsled race by a slim margin. Then my stupid laptop crashes. I hate my computer. It used to be Grandpa's, and I have to use his password to get on the Internet and so I'm always having to type in "Old Hot Cat" and it sucks.

I need to do something about Benny. I need to get a North Pottsboro phone book and look up his address. Then maybe I'll write him a letter in which I will mention that book *Down the Road*. Better yet, I'll give the letter to Reni. And she can stick it secretly in his locker.

I go to bed earlier than usual and miss watching *Nova* on TV with Grandpa. Ha ha. His favorite show, my biggest pain. I fall right to sleep because I have finally decided I am going to write something to Benny in the morning.

In the night I dream I go to my house on Cinnamon Street. Benny McCartney is standing in the doorway at the back of the house. Everything is dark. The tree next to the house casts a tangled web of shadows across Benny's face. He's holding the key to the house. He swings it in his hands and then he unlocks the back door and I go in alone. A feeling of terror creeps over me. The lights are on in all the rooms. They are too bright. My eyes hurt. I walk from the kitchen into the dining room, the living room, and then I come to the downstairs bedroom. The door is shut and I don't want to open it. No, I keep on saying. No, I am not going to open it. No. No. No.

What a dumb dream. I wake up out of it trembling when Grandpa's alarm goes off in their bedroom next to mine. Grandpa meant to set the alarm for 8:30 in the morning and instead he set it for 3:08 in the middle of the night. Grandma says she's gonna kill him, but then I hear them giggling and laughing in there, so I guess Grandpa will still be around in the morning.

When I get up at seven, I look at the card and envelope I was going to use and I decide my letter idea is totally lame. I can't even be sure of the name of the book. Maybe it was *In the Road* and not *Down the Road*. After that dream, do I even want to send any letter? For Reni's sake, I decide to ask Henderson, who is so good with words, to write something for me. Even though it's early, I text him. "Please, Hen?" I write.

He texts me back. "OK, Thumb."

So after school I go over to the South Pottsboro Public Library and there Henderson is, leaning over a pile of books. He must be working on a sad "treatise" (his word for "report") because his face, which usually has a wondrous stargazing look about it, today has, I don't know, maybe just a blank look about it. Henderson slides a paper across the table at me. It says:

Dear Benny,
I hope I will not bore you
With how totally, totally I adore you.
The cute way you have of talking,
The funny way you have of walking.
Please do not feel that I am stalking
You.
Love, Guess who???

"Wow, Henderson," I go, "this is awesome. I'll buy you a latte. Or a double latte or whatever you want, unless you get another free gift certificate, in which case I will definitely help you use it." Henderson usually welcomes all writing requests. He wrote one of the letters for Reni to Justin Bieber, but we think it got stuck with the other four in the lost and missing mail warehouse in Teaneck, New Jersey.

"You baffle me, Thumb," he says, looking out the

window at the snow falling. Clearly the snow is bothering Henderson or else it's something earth-shattering he's discovered about black holes or dying galaxies. I don't want to tell him that the note he wrote doesn't capture what I'm feeling. This Benny feeling is something else. Something *really* baffling.

Henderson is wearing his favorite green and gray flannel shirt that has been washed and washed so many times, it makes him look like an overly fuzzed teddy bear. A volcano-loving, poetry-crazed flannel teddy bear in wire-rimmed glasses. Every Christmas, he gets flannel shirts from everybody, even Annais, and he gets so happy about it. The weird thing is, I had another strange dream last night in which Benny delivered a pizza to my door, wearing one of Henderson's plaid flannel shirts. I mean, this is just off the map.

I sit down next to Henderson and lean my elbow on the library table. Soon we start talking about the possible crush and the pizza note. I don't tell Henderson about Frosty the Snowman and how much I did truly love him when I was six years old even though he melted at the end of the movie. I don't tell Henderson how much I wanted to squeeze and hug that snowman and how I even wanted to kiss his funny crooked mouth. I usually can tell Henderson anything, but I don't want him to know how mixed up I am about all this. I don't want him to know how lost I feel. Like I'm in a blizzard.

But Henderson is very sweet and listens quietly when I say, "It's possible I'm in love with Benny. I mean, there is something pulling me toward him. It's really strong. Reni says it must be love. Reni thinks so. Reni's sure."

"My sister actually doesn't know very much about love," says Henderson. "She harbors hope for this Bieber character."

Henderson stretches his hand across his face and then he sighs. And I think again about that note from Benny that said, *I am your biggest fan.* Those words are beginning to make little ripples and tugs on the wheels of confusion inside me. Frosty the Snowman dances across my closed eyes for a moment. He smiles and tilts his head. Then he disappears over the horizon. And I look up and see that in South Pottsboro, it's snowing outside again.

Chapter Eleven

My luck or what, Grandpa is getting into scrap-booking. "He's very adaptive for his age. Most seniors resist new hobbies. It's all in your attitude," Grandma says, doing a string of windmill stretches in the kitchen.

In the living room, Grandpa has these old photographs strewn across the coffee table. He's got these packages of sparkles and sprinkles and different colored pens to use for emphasis.

I think Grandpa is doing this just to make Grandma happy. He'll do anything to make Grandma happy. The only thing he won't do is buy himself new clothes. Grandma says he would staple up the holes in his pants and keep using them if she didn't step in. Once she tried to throw out a pair of million-year-old pajamas, but Grandpa found them in the condo Dumpster in the courtyard, and can you believe he pulled them out and kept wearing them? Finally, Grandma got rid of them by leaving them on the roof of the car when we were going to a local Laundromat cause our dryer was broken. We think they flew off somewhere around the intersection of Route 9 and Pottsboro Avenue.

I go over to sit on the couch, where Grandpa is using Krazy Glue. He's putting glitter around some of the photographs, like the one of me on the day I was born. I looked all wrinkly and red and clueless. My mom was holding me, but she had on a hospital mask, so now I can't see her face. I can just see her hair. It is a pretty yellow color.

"My mom had pretty hair," I say to my grandpa.

"Your mom was so beautiful," says Grandpa.

"I can't remember her hair. I can't remember her

face, either. I don't remember ever calling anybody Mom," I say.

"Don't you remember the time we went up to our cabin at Lake Mescopi? Remember when your mother rented the rowboat and took you around to all the islands there? You even stopped at the lake grocery store and bought a Fudgsicle."

"No," I say, "I can't remember any boat or any Fudgsicle." And then suddenly I get totally mad at my grandpa. I suddenly hate him. "I hate you, Grandpa," I shout and I get up and I go in my room and I slam the door.

I don't answer even when Grandma starts knocking and calling out, "Louise, darling. Sweetheart. Let your grandma give you a hug." Then my grandpa starts in and now they're both hammering away. But I don't answer. I just open the lid of my mom's jewelry box and let it play till it winds down.

Later I'm sitting at my desk looking at this card with a puppy on the front. It was from my dad. He's always calling us, but my grandma won't ever speak to him. He is always asking me to visit him, but then he doesn't ever exactly have a time that would fit with his schedule.

I did go to visit him last year. He has a new family in New York City. He has a stepdaughter around my age named Dearie, who plays the piano. Her mom was always going, "Dearie, dear, it's time to go to this recital or that performance." Chopin's 16th kiss my butt. Beethoven's 10th blah blah blah. In my opinion, any dude, living or dead, with a name like Wolfgang has got to be a major pain. I was like, "What else do you do around here?" And Dearie looked up at me with this what-are-you-talking-about? look on her face.

They do have this to-die-for apartment that looks like the honeymoon suite at the Marriott Hotel. I stayed there for two weeks. My dad was nice though, but very busy. When I left, he gave me this cute card with the puppy on the front. The puppy just, like, made me almost cry, it was sooo cute with this big red bow around his neck. Inside the card, there was a twenty-dollar bill. My dad had to go to work, so it was Dearie's mom who drove me to the airport. I didn't know what to call her. She wasn't my mom, but she was married to my dad. Riding in the car, we were pretty quiet. She kept asking me these dumb questions like did I have this book or did I know this person or that person. I answered every question with a yes or a no.

Then Dearie's piano teacher called on her cell, and she was going on about Dearie's piano technique. The whole time, I was staring at the adorable puppy card. That puppy was just looking at me with these big floppy ears and this soft puppy nose.

I pick up the card now and stare at it. Maybe it's the red bow or maybe it's his dopey ears, but for some reason that puppy just about wrings my freaking heart.

Chapter Twelve

Reni has been trying to learn how to draw. She has a pad full of sketches of shoes and cell phones and stuff. She's been drawing lots of pictures of Justin Bieber too and Annais has been calling her "a menace to society." Meanwhile, Henderson says he's fully analyzed the handwriting on the pizza letter and he has an idea who may have written it. He's coming over to discuss it.

"Henderson's on his way here," I say to my grandma and grandpa as they leave to go to a town planning meeting.

"Oh, wonderful!" says Grandma. "That boy is such a hoot. I love the way he reads everything from cereal boxes to Shakespeare. In my opinion, he's got what it takes. He'll probably grow up to be the president of the United States."

"No," I say, "Henderson doesn't want to be president. He wants to be secretary of state."

"See what I mean?" says Grandma, smiling. She leans back through the door and says, "Under several layers of dork, there lies a truly cool young man in Henderson."

Grandpa looks at her with great admiration. "My goodness, baby doll, you talk just like one of the kids. Doesn't she?"

"Uh, not really," I say, waving good-bye, double-time waves. As soon as I close the door, I start thinking about the Hen. He was there when Merit M started tripping me in the halls a couple of months ago. I'm not kidding you. Because of his messenger job, he was there. (Reni wants to know *how* he does all this. Come on, she says, he's a spy. He knows people. How does HE end up with a job like that? Come on, think about it.) I had just fallen on my face in the hall at school and

I was looking at the red and white tile floor up close, real close. Somebody gave me a hand. It was Hen.

Then he went with me to my geology class after that. We were studying the Mount St. Helens volcano that day. I told the teacher Henderson was my cousin visiting from Santa Fe, New Mexico.

And he loved that class. (I know. Henderson loves *everything*. But he really loved this class.) Now he studies all volcanoes, especially Mount St. Helens. And since then, he's been full of statistics about how many citizens croaked that day and how many people were buried up to their necks in volcanic ash and all that.

When Henderson comes in the door, he's starving, of course. I look at him and immediately I throw open the fridge, but there's squat in there for food.

"We'll have to order a pizza," I say, smiling.

"My stomach would not be in opposition to a double cheese, double anchovies, double pine nuts, extra large," Henderson says. (*Opposition* is one of his favorite words.)

"Done," I go, reaching into the antique Charlie Brown cookie jar, where my grandma and grandpa keep the pizza money for me. I don't even have to look up the pizza phone number; it's programmed into my cell. My Palomeeno's Pizza ticket has been punched so many times, I'll probably get a free pizza every six months for the rest of my life.

Henderson gets all comfy in my grandpa's chair, reading a book called *Benjamin Franklin: The Man and the Myth*. In the last couple of weeks, Henderson's buzz cut has started to grow out a little. He's laying his head back under Grandpa's reading lamp. I think it's cool that Henderson knows everything there is to know about Benjamin Franklin. He says his dad has a friend who is related to Benjamin Franklin and who was handed down through the ages an actual pair of Benjamin Franklin's underwear. With some of Henderson's stories, I'm like, "Yeah right. Whatever." The light is falling across Henderson's face, making him look ninety percent less geek and kind of, sweetly, sort of . . . I don't know.

"We're having a lunar eclipse next week," he says. "At three in the morning, we'll be able to see the earth's shadow on the moon. I'm planning on camping out in the backyard with a bunch of books and fourteen sandwiches."

"You better make that fifteen, Hen. You don't want to run out early and starve later," I say. "And, um, by the way, what did you decide about Benny's letter? I mean does the handwriting back up the facts?"

"Oh," he says, looking down. "The letter, um, well, I'm not totally sure yet. I mean, I can't say right now. I mean, well, I need more time and more information." He looks at the floor and then he puts the book up in front of his face again and starts reading.

My phone rings and it's Reni. "Hey ho," she goes. "Hey ho, what's up?"

"Oh, Hen is here and he's hungry and I'm going to order a pizza for him," I say.

"Aha!! Great!! Perfect!! I think you're gonna make it to the Spring Fling Dance after all, but you've got to be more aggressive. You're waffling. Put on that new gorgeous green dress," says Reni. "Now."

"I'm waffling?" I say.

"Yes, you are. But no more. Okay? Now, when Benny comes to the door with the pizza and you're wearing that dress, he'll *have* to notice you."

"What?" I say.

"Do you want to go to the Spring Fling Dance?"

"Yes."

"All right, then. Do it."

"Henderson," I say, shutting my cell and taking a deep breath. "I'm going to put on my new green dress so Benny will see me in it."

Henderson is still reading. He doesn't look up from his book. "Well, if you're looking to dazzle him, I guess," he says.

"I am, Henderson. I *do* want to dazzle him. I want to be dazzling." I spin around the room. Henderson is hidden again behind Ben Franklin's face on the cover of the book with his wire-rimmed Ben Franklin glasses and his funny little Ben Franklin two-hundred-year-old smile. Before I met Henderson, I thought Ben Franklin was that store on Main Street that sells notebooks and doodads and stuff.

I don't really have time to get the whole outfit together. Forget the crown and the shoes. I am pretty hyper now. I'm throwing clothes around my room. I feel a great need to do five somersaults, a couple of flips, and a major handspring. In this dress! Right. The buzzer is ringing and I'm so nervous, my hands are, like, flying all around me like a couple of lost birds. I have the green dress on, but for shoes, I'm still wearing my Day-Glo red plastic Crocs my grandma got me at Shaw's last week.

I rush out into the living room and take a quick turn. Oh, I love this dress! (My flips are begging me. My cartwheels are crying. Do one. Do one.) Oh, okay, I do one beautiful perfect cartwheel over the rug. My heart sings for one moment. I land on my feet right in front of Hen, so close I can barely breathe. Henderson is standing there stock-still. Ben Franklin is lying on the rug, staring up at us in a wise, smiling, 1700s way.

"Thumb," Henderson says, looking down at me.

"What?" I say. "The pizza is here! Come on."

"Oh, Thumb," he says again. "I've never seen . . . I can't believe . . ." He follows me with his eyes. He does not take his eyes off me.

"Henderson," I say, "what? The pizza's here."

I skip to the hall and open the door. Then smack in my face, there Benny is. He's in the hall, taking the pizza out of its warm little padded pizza case. After all this time, I look up at him.

And then Henderson comes up beside me and takes the pizza and goes, "Thanks, Benny. Keep the change. That'll be all." And he takes my hand and pulls me away from the door and shuts it. He sets the pizza on the coffee table.

Then I go, "Henderson?"

And he goes, "What?"

And I go, "What?"

And he goes, "What?"

And I go, "Henderson?"

And he goes, "What? I was hungry. That's all."

And then my cell rings and it's Reni again. I go into my room and I slam the door. I flop down on my bed and stare at the ceiling. Reni says, "Well, did Benny like the dress?"

"Um, I don't know," I say. "I'm not sure."

"You can't be serious," says Reni. My head is still spinning. I feel like I just swallowed a butterfly upside down. Then Reni starts blabbing on about some movie we want to go see next week. I listen for a while and I start to melt into the words. Then I join in. We blab for a while. Reni and I are good at that. We blab on for a long time. It gets dark outside. Very dark.

When my grandma and grandpa come home, I go back in the living room and see that the double cheese, double anchovies, double pine nuts, extra large pizza is sitting there on the coffee table untouched. And where is Henderson? Disappeared. Gone. Vanished.

Chapter Thirteen

My grandma just took me for my yearly checkup with Dr. Birpkin. He told me I've hit a plateau in my growing. He charged us money, but he didn't do anything about my being small. "Be patient," he said, slinging his stethoscope over his shoulder. I was thinking, "How about I'll *be* a patient and you *be* a doctor and *do* something about my height." I mean, what are doctors for?

Now my grandma and I are driving home in silence. At a red light, my grandma says, "Remember when you used to write poems? Remember when you used to say things that were so poetic I used to jot them down in a notebook? Now you're all angry and bristly, honey." She reaches out and squeezes my hand.

"You mean bristles like on a hairbrush?" I say.

"Well, yes, kind of," she says.

I don't answer. I'm never speaking to anyone again. Seriously.

When we're walking in the door of the apartment, Grandma throws her purse on the couch and says to Grandpa, "You know what I discovered in the basement today while I was down there sweeping?"

"What?" says Grandpa.

"Asbestos," says my grandma.

Grandpa raises his eyebrows and looks over at me like he and I are a unit, like a washer and dryer set, and Grandma is a stove way on the other side of the room. "Where, baby doll?" he says, still smiling at me.

Grandma gives Grandpa a you-didn't-take-out-the-garbage-so-now-I'm-going-to-have-you-arrested look. She puts her hands on her hips and says, "I was down in the basement this morning and suddenly I noticed there is asbestos around all the pipes down there."

"How do you know for sure, Cecile? It's wrapping that has been there for a long time. You can't tell by looking at it. Anyway, it's better if you don't disturb it," he says. When Grandpa stops calling my grandma baby doll and starts in with Cecile, you know it's serious.

"Oh, I can tell," she goes. "We've got to do something about it now."

"I see," says Grandpa. "You are planning to rile up everybody in the building. Everybody will be up in arms and we don't even know if it *is* asbestos." Baby doll and honey bear have disappeared and it's Phil and Cecile heading into the ring.

I go out into the hall again, with Grandpa saying, "You don't know, Cecile."

And then Grandma says, "Oh yes, I do, Phil."

I decide to go up on the roof. There's a terrace and in warm weather a garden, and last summer Mr. Anderson grew twelve watermelons up here. Now, since it's the end of March, snow is melting all over the

Pottsboro area, exposing everything. On the roof, all the furniture is dumped upside down and rosebushes are wrapped up in crummy burlap. There's junk thrown around, like old beer cans and newspapers, and there are chunks of old snow and ice that look glacial, like they're never in a million years going to melt.

I stand at the guardrail that goes around the top of the roof. I look down at all the cars and people below. You could easily get blown right off this roof if you didn't hold on. When I look straight down the side of the building, my stomach turns over and a weird, tingly, scary feeling goes through me. I guess Thelma and Louise drove off that cliff in the movie because if they didn't, they would have had to go to jail forever. "They wanted to be free," Grandma always explains to me after the movie is over. "They wanted freedom from their lives."

"That's why they killed themselves?" I always say back.

And Grandma always says, "Yes."

I get out my cell and call Reni, but she doesn't answer. I sit up here on this slippery-wet, rusty, upside-down chair, and the wind knocks me around. I look off into the distance and see the buildings at the edge of the horizon stretching away. I can see ice cracking and buckling up on the melting river. I can see old snow in piles dripping into large puddles of water.

I need to talk to Reni. I dial her cell again. Reni, where are you? Come on. Come on, pick up. I need you. I text her and get nothing back. Then I keep hitting redial and redial on my cell until finally, twenty minutes later, she answers.

"Hey ho, Reni," I go. "Where have you been?"

"Hey ho, I've just been killing my brother. He is driving me crazy," Reni says.

"Oh, good," I say, "kill him for me too. He's been acting sooo weird. Does he have the flu or something? He turned into a psychopath overnight. I mean, what's his problem?"

"I don't know. My mom called him 'utterly listless' today," says Reni. "He's moaning and mooning around and staring out the window all the time."

"He's probably dreaming up a new novel," I say.

"No, this is different. I mean, if he's a spy, maybe

his agency fired him or something," says Reni. "By the way, word is out at North."

"What?" I say. "Go on."

"Word is out that Benny got a letter. Your letter! Only problem was by mistake I ripped a bumper sticker Benny had pasted over those air slats when I stuffed that letter in his locker."

"Oh no," I say.

"No, it's fine. I don't think he cared because now Benny's all flustered and honored and embarrassed and proud and curious all at once. He's trying to figure out who sent the letter. He wrote on his locker in big bold letters *WHO ARE YOU?*"

"I'm gonna faint," I say. "I got to get off this roof." I start running down the steps to the hallway. "Reni, help. What am I gonna do?" I start going on and on about how scared I am and how freaked I am and how I'm not ready for this, and suddenly I realize I'm talking to nobody at all. My cell has died. It always dies at *the* moment. I hate my cell.

When I get back to our apartment, my grandma is on the phone with an asbestos testing service. She's saying, "Well, we'd like to get this done immediately." And Grandpa is in the living room doing Tai Chi. He's standing in the middle of the room in these dorky sweatpants and a black Chinese T-shirt. He's got a headband around his head and he's standing there moving slowly, with his arms out as if he's about to lift up to the ceiling. I'm like, "Move over, Grandpa. I need to watch TV. Where's the suitcase?"

He doesn't answer. He turns carefully, listening to this weird Chinese music. "Grandpa," I go. He smiles but then he makes a hushing motion and brings his arms out in front of him like he's holding a huge beach ball. I'm sure we will hear from that lady downstairs any minute. She seems to know when Grandpa puts on his Tai Chi "duds," as he calls them.

I go in my room and I close the door. I am so freaked. What am I gonna do? There is no way I could ever say two words to Benny now. This is too huge. This has gone way beyond me.

Chapter Fourteen

At the grocery store, Grandma tells me I can put whatever I want in the cart. "That's called carte blanche,"
says Grandpa.

Grandma laughs, "Good one, honey bear."

Grandpa is pushing the cart. Grandma says he's the
kind of guy who always takes over the shopping cart at
the grocery. She goes, "Some husbands follow their
wives around looking dazed, but your grandpa takes
charge at the grocery store."

In the dairy aisle, Grandpa starts making a truck sound. "Rummm, rummmm, rummm," he goes, pushing the cart around me. And Grandma says, "Oh, he's such a child."

And I whisper to him as he passes me, "Grow up, Grandpa."

We move to the cereal aisle, and Grandma and Grandpa are reading labels. "After we're done, I'm going over to Reni's. Okay?" I go, gently putting a puffy, airy, delightful package of Cheez Doodles into the cart.

"Maybe you should go to the town offices and get your last name changed to Elliot," says my grandma, looking over the tops of her glasses at me. Then she bumps her forehead against mine and rubs my nose with her nose.

I look down at the Cheez Doodles. "Can I take these along? I'm starved."

"Sure, pal," goes Grandpa. "But I was going to teach you some Tai Chi this afternoon."

I am thinking about Merit Madson and Janie Brevette. "Does Tai Chi have karate chops in it, where you get to knock someone to the floor and they beg for mercy?"

"Oh no," Grandpa says looking at me like he's president of the Pottsboro Worrying Club.

As soon as we're through the checkout lane, I grab the Doodles and I'm history. The thing is, Reni has found out the actual address and phone number of Benny McCartney. This is very cool news. She got it out of Annais last night. Not in an open sort of way, but in a brilliant underhanded Reni sort of way. Reni is definitely chairman of the board of totally awesome, reliable, way cool best friends.

I trolley over there and hop off right at Nutmeg. Thank goodness the trolley is free and it's not a long ride from South P to North P. (Okay, so the old town planner has done a few good things in his life.)

When I get in the door at the Elliots', the smell of the house tells me in a weird way that I'm home. "I'm here, Reni," I shout as I open the front door and climb the stairs toward her room. When I get to the top, I find Henderson lying on his back across the landing with his head drooping down on the last step. He has his hand over his heart and robot tears in his eyes.

Reni is up in the hall and she calls out, "What are you doing? Mom, Henderson is dying and he's in Thumbelina's way. Move. She needs to get by."

"Wait," says Henderson, "this is a great moment. My whole novel hangs on this scene. Bear with me, Thumb, I'm working out my plot. This is the moment when the dude realizes he's really a robot. And this is the scene in which he realizes he will never be able to have the princess from Jupiter because of it. And he loves her."

"But he's a robot, Henderson. What does a robot know about love?" says Reni. "Now move over."

"This is the tragedy of it," says Henderson, sitting up. "Thumb, will you go over and stand in the doorway for one minute and be Zandra so I can see your expression as Zandra becomes aware of the death of the robot?"

"Later, Henderson," says Reni, "we are in a hurry. Please?"

Part of me really wants to be Zandra for Henderson, even though Reni is totally annoyed. She pulls me along and I step around him and go into her room. And the whole time I'm in there I'm thinking of Henderson lying out there on the floor, dying of a broken heart. A part of me thinks Henderson is kind of . . . I don't know, and of course at the same time, Reni's right, he's a major pain.

When Reni's ready to leave, I head back downstairs. Henderson is standing in the hallway and doesn't say anything for the first time in his life. He just stands there looking at me. "Hey, Hen," I go.

I'm wondering if Henderson has been to a doctor lately. He is acting seriously off the wall. His eyes look big and soft and, for some reason, browner than usual, as if there's a sadness in them that has made the brown deeper and more layered.

Then Reni comes downstairs with her spotted-cow backpack already on her back. She's wearing pink tights, a pink wool skirt, and a pink sweatshirt that says, BROTHER FOR SALE. WILL TAKE ANY OFFER.

"Later, Henderson," I shout as we go out the door. "We're going to sell magazine subscriptions for Annais. Call me." He just stands there looking tall and un-Hendersonly quiet, leaning his head against the wall and staring at me like I'm a puzzle with a piece missing.

"What's Benny's address?" I say, ripping open the Cheez Doodles and offering the bag to Reni. She grabs a big handful and we both start going crazy chowing down. Reni's eating even faster than me, and when I look over at her, I realize I shouldn't have brought the Doodles at all. "Still down two pounds?" I say.

"Yep," says Reni, taking another humongous handful of Doodles. "This is just a breather. I'm down three pounds now." Reni wants to lose twenty pounds before the Spring Fling Dance. She has bright orange Cheez Doodle fuzz on her cheeks and on the tip of her nose.

We come to the corner of Cilantro just after Marjoram and then we make a quick left onto Peppercorn.

"Does Benny live on Peppercorn?" I say.

"Yup," says Reni. "He actually lives at 152 Peppercorn Street."

"Oh," I say and I feel a little tug of something weird. These tugs are starting to bug me. "It's so near my old house. He lives near Cinnamon Street. I didn't know that."

It has grown windy, and the sky is turning a cloudy dark gray. This seemed like a cheery neighborhood a few minutes ago, but now it has a gloomy, windy, abandoned feeling about it. I'm very nervous and I'm almost wishing we could turn around and not do this. Not yet.

Reni looks so bright and pink in the dark stormy air and she keeps bopping along. We pass a couple of middle school kids playing Frisbee in the empty street. One of the kids is wearing a clown wig and a red clown nose.

"I guess the circus came to town," whispers Reni.

"Ha ha," I say, but then a shiver goes through me and I button up my jacket. We pick up the pace. Some of our papers blow away and we have to chase them. We hear a dog barking behind a fence. I hear the sound of thunder rumbling in the distance. A few blocks later, I turn around and I see the circus clown by himself now. His collar is turned up on his striped clown jacket and his face is tucked behind it in the darkness. "Is he following us?" I say.

"I doubt it," goes Reni. There are puddles of water everywhere and we have to jump over one that's shaped like a mountain range, like Mount Everest melting.

Finally we get to 152 Peppercorn.

It's a nice house. I mean, it has a glassed-in porch at the front with a screened porch above it. All the houses in this area are similar. That's one of the things Grandma doesn't like about our green house on Cinnamon Street. "They're cheap tract houses from the 1940s war years over there. They aren't well built," Grandma always says. And then her eyes will fill up with tears and she'll look out the window and won't answer anybody. Not even when Grandpa goes and holds her in his old hairy arms for ten minutes.

I don't like the looks of this house. For some reason, I do not want to go up on the porch. I feel like running. Reni gets ready to knock on the glass door. I stand on the sidewalk and then I want to turn away. I feel sick and I need to go home. Home. Where is my home? Which home? Reni, don't.

Reni knocks on the door and then waits and then pushes the bell. In a few minutes, we hear padded feet in slippers shuffling across the floor and then someone, a woman, comes to the door. She doesn't really understand what we are trying to sell. She doesn't care much about astrology magazines. She'll show it to her son, she says. Okay. She takes the order form and closes the door.

The whole time, I have been standing behind Reni, out of sight, but just as the woman closes the door, I look at her. Just a tiny, quick glimpse. I remember something. Mrs. McCartney's face. She was in my house on Cinnamon Street. She was there.

Reni and I stand in the darkening yard. The wind blows gray clouds over the rooftops, and cloud shadows stream across the street. When we turn around, the clown is sitting on somebody's wooden fence opposite us. He's mostly hidden by bushes and all I can really see of him are his big, dark floppy shoes swinging back and forth. We start walking faster. Then we turn on to Coriander Street.

We hear more rumbling far away, spring thunder, and it makes me feel breathless. I am still trying not to think about Lake Mescopi and what my grandpa said. I am still trying and trying and trying not to remember riding in a rowboat with my mom. I'm trying not to remember the swirling water, the dark trees moving against the sky, the wind. I'm trying not to imagine the oars dipping into the water, the boat gliding forward, my mom and me sitting in the middle of the lake when it started to rain. We sat there in the boat together watching the rain hit the surface of the dark lake.

Why did my father decide to leave my mother and me and go live in New York City and be Dearie's step-father instead? Is Dearie a better daughter? Is she smarter and prettier and taller than me? The rain started falling harder and harder. My mom pulled me against her. Her sweater was wet. Her arms were wet. I looked down at her shoes and saw that they were sitting in a pool of water at the bottom of the boat. We sat there for forty-five minutes in the middle of the lake for no reason at all until the sky quit raining and the sun came out and she rowed me to the grocery store and bought me a Fudgsicle.

Chapter Fifteen

Grandpa comes to the kitchen this morning wearing a nerdy baseball cap that he got from the condo's Lost and Found in the basement. It says on the front, DON'T EVER FORGET CHICKEN MAN.

"Who is Chicken Man?" I ask my grandpa.

"Don't know," says Grandpa, smiling and doing a dance. "Fits perfectly, though."

Grandma says, "Honey bear, you're gonna catch something nasty one of these days and be sorry."

Grandpa settles the cap lower down around his ears. "I got something nasty when I caught you, and I'm still not sorry, baby doll."

Grandma rolls her eyes and puts her hands on her hips. Grandpa sits down at the counter and starts eating something that looks like somebody's science experiment. Seriously.

Then the door buzzer goes off for downstairs, and Grandma goes to the little speaker at the wall and calls out, "Who is it?"

And a tinny, tiny cartoon voice calls back, "Mailman here. Package delivery."

"I'll be right down," says Grandma, flying out the door. She comes back a few minutes later all screechy and excited with a package in her arms. "A package for Louise!" she says.

"For me?" I say, pulling up my recycled milk bottle socks that always slip down below my ankles. "What is it?"

"A package?" says Grandpa. "From a boyfriend?"

Grandma swats Grandpa with a flyer from the Organic Owl that she picked up when she was out in the hall. She says, "Honey bear, *très* uncool."

I look at the package closer. It has no return address. No sign of who sent it at all.

"Aren't you going to open it, pal?" says Grandpa.

"Not in front of you, Grandpa," I say, and I go into my room and shut the door behind me. Grandma and Grandpa just stand there as I close the door, looking baffled and curious, like two matching rabbits.

I look at the package again. Hmmm. Nobody I know would send me anything. I'm basically on a solo mission here in South Pottsboro. I don't know one single person who might send me a package unannounced, unless it would be Merit Madson sending me something spooky. Last fall when Torrie M's house got papered, the gymnastics team first sent her a case of toilet paper, sixteen rolls, and a note that said, *You're full of bull, but we love you still! Great double saltos. See ya tonight!!* They loved her double saltos, but they hated mine. I was just "tickled pink," as Grandma would say. The gymnastics team was always doing stuff in the true team spirit, like going out for ice cream in a group or getting together and pushing, shoving, bashing, kicking, scaring somebody off the team for no freaking reason.

I pick up the package and shake it. Pottsboro postal workers say you should not open mysterious packages; they could explode or something. Maybe I should just throw it out the window.

Finally, I start pulling on the brown paper wrapping. I wish my grandpa was right. I wish a boy had sent me something. I suppose miracles do happen. Grandma says they do. She'll go, "Well, it will take a miracle, but we're coming in on a wing and a prayer." If a boy sent me a package, I would fly over the freaking moon and die. Reni would have to write my obituary and I hope she would omit the part about how I once left a pair of my soaking-wet cross trainers in a box under the backseat in their car. Those shoes grew moldy and stank so badly that Mrs. Elliot had to have the car cleaned professionally.

I tear off the front of the package and start working at the rows of Scotch tape, and finally I make an opening in the brown paper and I can reach in and feel the shiny smooth surface of a book. I slide it out and put it on my lap. It says, *Thumbelina: A Fairy Tale*. On the cover is a beautiful tiny girl standing among flowers . . . roses, violets, tulips, and lilacs. I open up the book and begin reading. "Once there was a very tiny girl who was small enough to sit in the palm of your hand and her name was Thumbelina." A wave of something so sweet washes over me and I hold the book against me for a moment and close my eyes.

Chapter Sixteen

I spot Reni and Henderson at the Pottsboro Pumpkin Mall. This mall was built on the site of an old pumpkin farm, so all the shops and restaurants in here have names like the Pumpkin Seed and PaPa's Pumpkin and stuff like that. At Halloween, of course, this mall is ridiculous. That's when Grandma and Grandpa come over here to represent the town planning board, dressed up as Mr. and Mrs. Peter Peter Pumpkin Eater.

Reni and Henderson don't see me yet, but I can see them at the Party Pumpkin Shop buying stuff for Annais's art-opening celebration. Reni is carrying a bunch of birthday hats, and Henderson has packages of balloons in his hands. It's not Christmas or anything like that, but Reni is wearing her goofy headband with the reindeer antlers that stick up. It's so Elliot family funny. I just start laughing over here. Henderson keeps taking the antlers and putting them on his head. Henderson looks really dorky in the antlers.

"Hey ho, Reni! Hen!" I say. Then I just kind of go over and hang with them, even though I'm only supposed to be here to get Grandpa a package of Tums.

Henderson buys the balloons and hats and then we three sit for a moment on a bench installed by the town planning board across from the Party Pumpkin. This one is named the Bill Bentley Bench.

"Word is out around North," says Reni, "that Benny knows who sent the letter."

"Really?" I go. And then I gulp quietly.

"Yeah, and he's got this silly smile on his face when you see him in the hall."

"Really?" I say calmly, but inside, it feels like I'm falling off a mountain. I gulp again. "Are you sure he knows?" Then I think about the book I got yesterday. I even saved the sweet brown paper the package was wrapped in. There was no note inside, but I studied the way the sender wrote my name: *Louise Terrace*. I noticed the way the letters were made, the cute way the *E* was tucked so close to the *R*s. I usually can't keep much from Henderson and Reni, so I blurt out, "Somebody sent me this sweet book."

"Oh!!! It must have been Benny! The pizza stalker!!! He strikes again!!! Oh my gosh. You're so lucky! This proves it, and he's so cute," squeals Reni.

"Gee," goes Henderson, "you're kidding. A book? Benny? I didn't know he knew how to read."

"Wow," goes Reni, elbowing Henderson. "Amazing. Incredible. How romantic to send you a book! What was it called?"

"*How I Survived My Frontal Lobotomy* by Benny McCartney," says Henderson.

"Oh, never mind, you guys. I shouldn't have told you," I say. "Forget it."

Henderson takes the reindeer antlers off and puts them on my head. "There's your crown, Thumbelina," he says. And I smile.

"Henderson will be so much happier," says Reni, "when he finds out if he got accepted to that writer's camp he's trying for."

"Oh, I forgot about the writer's camp. Is that what's been bothering you?" I say.

"Yep," goes Henderson. "That's what's bothering me."

"Yeah," says Reni, "he's entered his application. He wrote this really long essay on bloodletting in the time of Napoleon. All the most talented kids in the country who want to be writers will be there. If you get in, it's full credit for the last part of the semester. You have to take some tests early on and it's a big deal."

"Wow, Henderson, that's awesome," I say. "If they knew what a cool, fabulous, great writer you are, they'd accept you in a snap. Wouldn't they, Reni?"

"Thanks," Henderson says, and he looks kind of wistful and puts his hands in his pockets.

We end up going to a store with tons of bumper stickers.

"Well," goes Reni, "if Benny spent money on a book for you, the least you can do is buy him a new bumper sticker since I wrecked his old one. You are gonna make it to the Spring Fling Dance, girl. I'm gonna get you there."

I bump my head against Reni's shoulder. I would have butted heads with her, but she's too far up there. We start going through the bumper stickers in a bin. Henderson wants me to get the one that says, KEEP HONKING. I'M RELOADING.

But I go, "No, Henderson. He doesn't have a car. This is for his locker."

We finally decide to get one that says, IF YOU LIVED IN YOUR CAR, YOU'D BE HOME BY NOW. We're going to cross out *car* and put in the word *locker* so it will say, "If you lived in your locker, you'd be home by now."

Henderson is frowning. He still has his hands in his pockets, and his glasses have slipped partway down his nose, so he looks kind of thoughtful, like a thirteen-year-old professor with a bothered poetic twist. I decide to get my grandma and grandpa a bumper sticker too. It says, THIS VEHICLE STOPS AT ALL GARAGE SALES.

As we leave the mall, Reni's wearing the antlers

again. We step out into the parking lot and I lock arms with Reni on one side and Henderson on the other. I lean my head against Henderson, and the warm fuzzy flannel of his shirt feels nice against my cheek. Suddenly a wave of something sweet pours over me. We pass a poster of Frosty the Snowman standing in front of the main door to the mall. Underneath Frosty, it says, SAY GOOD-BYE TO WINTER! SPRING SALE!! FIFTY PERCENT OFF EVERYTHING!! I feel a tiny melting glimmer of something.

Chapter Seventeen

I get in on the ground floor with everything the Elliots do. Sometimes I'll call Mrs. Elliot and say, "Mrs. Elliot, I'm going to the store, can I get anything for you? If you are making cookies, I can pick up the chocolate chips."

And she'll go, "You have great manners, Louise. I wish Reni was that polite. No, thank you, though. We're all set for supplies."

I'm so much a part of the Elliot family that when I hear they are hanging Annais's paintings at the gallery,

I show up on my own. I don't even wait for an invitation. Who needs an invitation when you are a true member of the family? The minute I get there, I start to help unload paintings. I don't need to be thanked. When you are part of a family, you are expected to help. Right?

Inside the gallery, Annais is standing in the middle of the room with Mrs. Elliot. They're both wearing matching flowery flowing dresses. "I want that painting over there," says Annais, pointing. Her black hair is long and so curly and it stands out around her body. When she moves her head, it follows her and swishes around her like a silky black shawl. Her mom nods.

Henderson is over in the far corner of the big empty room. He's on the floor, reading a book. Reni and I are leaning against the wall across the room. Reni has her drawing pad with her. "Here's a new sketch I did of Justin Bieber," she says. "I think I made him look like stir-fried mashed potatoes by mistake."

"No, Reni, it's nice," I whisper. "Hey, I thought of something problematic recently."

"What?" says Reni.

"It's possible Newton Mancini left the note. He delivers a lot of pizza to my door. He started asking me questions last night."

"Like what kind of questions?" goes Reni.

"Oh, he was asking if you and I were interested in participating in some walkathon. I didn't know he even knew we were friends."

"Really? I never thought of him. He's not bad, pretty cute actually," Reni says. And then she looks at me, shining with Reni sureness. "Uh. Nope. This note is a Benny McCartney deal. This is his style."

Suddenly the big wide gallery space makes me want to do a series of flips. I could do a string all across the room. I could throw in a handspring at the end. Oh, I miss my handsprings. No, I say to myself. No. No. No. I bite my fingers.

Annais has her thumb and arm out as she eyeballs where a painting should be hung. Then she glances over at me. Her voice echoes in the big room. "What are you whispering about? I hope you two are dropping this Benny nonsense. It's totally off the wall," she says, squinting now at the wall before her. "No pun intended, girls. Over to the left, Mom," she calls to Mrs. Elliot.

"Like this?" Mrs. Elliot calls back.

"Perfect," goes Annais.

Henderson looks up at me. He has a train-station expression on his face, the kind of expression people have when they're holding suitcases and are about to say good-bye and climb aboard. I don't know what he's been reading lately, but it seems to have done the impossible. Henderson has stopped smiling. "Thumb, did you know that before Roald Dahl wrote *Charlie and the Chocolate Factory*, he worked for the British government in Washington as a spy during World War II?"

"Really?" I say. "A spy?"

"So you see," he says, "someday I *can* be secretary of state and still write mysteries on the side."

"Cool," I say. "Did you like the part where the spoiled fat kid drowns in the chocolate?"

"It's my favorite part," Henderson says.

"Mine too," I say.

Reni looks at me looking over at Henderson and says, "Hey, by the way, speaking of chocolate, I had a box of Justin Bieber chocolates in the van. Each piece of candy had a *JB* on it. They're gone. Did you eat them, Henderson?"

"Well, *you* shouldn't be eating chocolate anyway," he says.

"What's all this stuff disappearing for? Speaking of spies, *you're* a spy. I know it. We'll find your attaché case after you've left town," says Reni.

Henderson looks confused. "What?" he says.

"Grrr," goes Reni. Then she slides back down the wall to the floor and whispers to me. "You have to be careful what you tell Henderson. He puts stuff in his novel. Remember that time our school took a field trip to the state capitol last year and I got my foot stuck in the space next to the elevator door and nobody could get my foot out? Finally the police came and the newspaper reporters, and our state senator came out and gave a speech while I was lying there on the floor with my foot stuck. Remember? Well, Henderson put that in his novel. In his book, it happened to some nerdy robot girl from planet Zing Zong. I was, like, super mad. I was going to sue Henderson, but my mom says you can't sue your brother."

"You probably would have lost anyway, Reni," I say.

"Yeah, you're right. Oh, I forgot to tell you. Yesterday I stuffed the new bumper sticker into Benny's locker," she says.

"You did?" I say.

"Yeah. I drew this little smiley face on it in the corner. It was so cute. It was my best smiley face."

"Did everything go okay this time?"

"Yeah, except that Benny saw me doing it."

"He saw you? Oh no," I whisper.

"Yeah, and he came over and saw the bumper sticker and he started laughing. He said it was really funny."

"Oh no. Did you tell him anything? I mean, about me?"

"No, but I gave him an invitation to the opening and he said he was planning on being there."

"Oh my gosh," I say in Reni's ear, "I feel dizzy. Why didn't you wait to put the bumper sticker in his locker till he wasn't around? I think I'm going to die."

"Don't worry so much," Reni says out loud now. "He isn't a snowman. He isn't going to melt and disappear."

"Speaking of snowmen," says Henderson from

across the room, "Thumb, do you know how to say *snowman* in French? It's *un bonhomme de neige*, which translates as 'a good man of snow.' If you ever want to hear the original French poem about a snowman that came before Frosty, I know it by heart."

Reni rolls her eyes at me. "Figures," she says.

By now Mrs. Elliot has hung up about three big messy-looking paintings. She's standing there with Annais in the middle of the room. I look around at the mushy, blurry paintings hanging on the walls, and Henderson's word comes to mind again. *Baffling, baffled, bafflement.*

"*My Dreams* has so much feeling in its abstraction, honey. It has *great* feeling. Oh, I'm so proud of you," Mrs. Elliot says, and she throws her big happy arms around Annais. "This is just the best show I've ever seen. Pablo Picasso, move over!"

Reni sits on the floor, looking down at one of her drawings. Then suddenly she gets up and starts to cross the room toward her mom. She's holding out her drawing. But halfway there Reni changes her mind. She closes the pad and slides back down to the floor.

Chapter Eighteen

It's that time of year in April when everybody is just waiting for spring and sunshine. So what do we get instead? A big, nasty, windy rainstorm. It's early afternoon and I'm coming back from the café and gallery. I'm on the Toot Toot Trolley again. Suddenly, I hear my cell ringing. It's in my backpack. Grandpa programmed my cell to play his favorite Beatles song.

"Your backpack is ringing," says the lady sitting next to me. "Cute song too," she says.

"Thanks," I say and start fumbling and rummaging in there. I hear a great whoosh of wind and rain and I pull my cell out and open it. "Hey, Reni," I go.

"Hey ho," says Reni. "Are you sitting down?"

"Yeah," I go.

"In a great big sturdy chair? Are you ready for this?"

"What? Reni, I'm sitting in a trolley seat. Yes, I'm ready," I say.

"Oh my gosh, I was vacuuming the hallway upstairs when we came back from the café. I went into Henderson's room and I'm standing there and suddenly I look on his shelf and I see this curly clown wig and this red clown nose and a clown jacket."

"What???" I say. "A striped jacket with big yellow pockets?"

"Yes," says Reni.

"Oh my gosh. Henderson has gone completely off the wall. I mean, what is he doing? That writer's camp has caused him to seriously go bananas. I don't know this kid anymore and he was, like, my best friend."

"I thought I was your best friend," she says.

"Oh, well, you were both my better than best. I mean, I could always tell Henderson anything. I mean, he knows everything. And now he has become a total lunatic. Look what he did when Benny was at my door with the pizza."

"I know," says Reni. "This spy thing keeps popping up. Well, to be fair, I guess he's major stressed. I have to say, he was nice today and mailed out two hundred invitations to Annais's opening celebration and he ended up helping my mom contact *The Pottsboro Shopping Guide* for a possible review. We're renting a microphone to have there. My mom loves testimonials and people getting up and talking and reading poems and stuff."

"It's gonna be great," I go. "I can't wait." And then an enormous gust of wind rushes across the sky and shakes every tree and building and it must have shaken all the air waves and signals that make cells work, cause Reni and I get cut off again. Honestly, is it me or do all cell phones die when you need them the most?

I spend the rest of the rainy, windy trip home thinking about Henderson wearing that clown suit and following us that day. Was he being protective and supportive in his old Henderson way? Or was he being demented and weird and looking for material for his next novel? Reni's right, he *is* always listening and watching for ideas to put in his books. He pauses in stores to listen to conversations. He watches people. He writes notes on a pad. On the other hand, maybe he was just being good old Henderson from planet Good Guy. It kind of makes me feel special that I have someone who would protect me like that. It feels kind of nice in a weird sort of way.

The trolley stops and I get out into the wind and rain and run down the street to our condo building. To be quite honest, I feel suddenly like I am in Henderson's latest novel. There are two guys in white puffy moon suits, wearing space helmets with breathing tubes, coming out of the basement door of our condo. They have on great big white gloves and they are carrying this little metal box. A lot of people from our condo are out on the street even though it's raining. My grandma is standing there in her vintage coat with her arms crossed, talking at a distance with one of the astronauts.

Have I been transported to some other planet?

"What is going on?" I say. "What's with the Star Wars stormtrooper dudes?"

Grandpa leans over toward me, and under his breath and out of the side of his mouth like some old-time detective in one of Henderson's old 1940s movies, he says, "Well, pal, your grandma won the battle. They're testing those wrappings around the furnace pipes for asbestos. If it is asbestos, it's been there for fifty years, so now we're going to disturb it and everyone living here. Your grandma's a pro."

The woman from downstairs comes at my grandpa with the pointed end of an umbrella. "Mr. Terrace," she says, "you do nothing but bungle things. These condos are our investment. What have you done now and why are these spacemen here?" He gives her a very sheepish smile and takes off into the crowd.

Me, I just sit down on the wet curb and watch the moon men waving their moon-suit arms around, and then in their big moon boots, they climb in their truck and drive away. I cross my arms and sigh, waiting to go back to my room upstairs, feeling like a party girl endlessly without a party.

Chapter Nineteen

It's close to the end of April and it's still raining. Once it was snow, then the temperature climbed above freezing, and the snow turned to rain. Either way, so much has been falling from the sky. It's a cold, gloomy South Pottsboro rain. Grandma says, "Oh, it's our big winter cleansing, honey. Think of all the old snow and dirty drainpipes that are being scrubbed and freshened and dressed up for spring." She says this in a very peppy way. I'm surprised she hasn't added her usual "Oh, don't you love the rain? Isn't life just full of magic!" Grandpa looks at her with a special forgiving smile and he stands with his hands clasped behind his back, as if he's about to surprise her with a bouquet of flowers.

Then suddenly his earpiece rings. Someone is actually calling my grandpa on his cell phone headset! At first Grandpa hardly knows what to do. He gets all flustered. It turns out to be the angry lady downstairs who wants him to explain about the men in moon suits. "It was just a test," Grandpa says, kind of shouting to be heard. "They just took some pieces away to test. They'll let us know in ten days or so. Well, if it tests positive for asbestos, we'll just have it removed. That's all. No, no, it's fine. No worries. What, me worry?" he says, laughing.

Then my grandpa gets real quiet while the lady announces loud enough so that I can hear that she is selling her condo. She doesn't want to live with any asbestos pipes.

Grandpa shouts back, not because he's angry, but like he's never gotten the hang of telephones. Come to think about it, telephones were probably just being invented when Grandpa was little. Before that, I think his parents had to communicate with smoke signals. "No need to sell now," Grandpa shouts, smiling. "It will probably be fine."

I watch the rain out the window and I am thinking I will have to bring an umbrella to Annais's big celebration tonight. I'm already planning my "getting ready" schedule. First I'll take a shower. I bought some awesome pumpkin pie shampoo at the Pampered Pumpkin. Then I will put on lip gloss, a touch of blush, freshen up my nail polish, slip on my shoes (my dumb child's-size-12 white patent leather ones.) And then *the* dress and the crown of rosebuds and violets. Okay. Fine. I know. It's over the top. But I *feel* over the top. And besides, Benny sent me the book *Thumbelina: A Fairy Tale*. I can't show up looking just like any other ordinary girl. I should show up looking like a princess. I mean over-the-top or not, a person must come to accept the true responsibility of their destiny. Right?

Just to make sure of everything, I call Reni. "Hey, Reni," I go. "I think you're right. I am starting to crush Benny. It's happening. I mean, who wouldn't love someone who could send a book like that? That book shows that person knows me all the way down to my toes. It's my favorite book in the whole world."

"Well, it's about time," goes Reni. "Opportunities like this don't grow on trees."

"So, Reni," I say, "what's everybody wearing tonight?"

"Mom says we should all wear whatever we want. Be creative. Wear anything you want."

"Your mom is so great." I go, "She's just sooo my mom too. You know what I mean?"

Reni goes, "Annais is wearing this gorgeous beaded dress. It's like flapper girl goes New Age. OMG, it's so cool. I bet it weighs ten pounds. I'm wearing my pink Easter dress even though Henderson says I look like the Easter Bunny's daughter in it."

"I didn't realize the Easter Bunny *had* a daughter," I say.

"Henderson is wearing a plaid flannel shirt and jeans," says Reni.

"Really?" I go, "How unusual. Ha ha. Do you think I can wear my new dress?"

"Of course you can. It's a creative dress night. You should wear it. You know Benny will be there. This is it."

It takes me hours to get ready and we only have one bathroom, so when I'm all done with my shower and nails and my hair and everything, I step out of there in a cloud of steam, and there's Grandpa looking all desperate, hopping up and down from foot to foot, waiting to get in. "You know your grandpa has that wild loose bladder," says Grandma, folding her arms as I pass her in the hall. This is my life.

Finally the dress is on. The shoes are on. My hair is blown dry. I look in the mirror and I add the crown of flowers. Then when I'm all done, I go out into the living room, and Grandma and Grandpa are standing there with cameras. Two different kinds. There's Grandpa's old Nikon with a big silver flash on top, and Grandma's little digital camera. They both start shooting away.

"Oh, isn't it just lovely. Oh, Louise, I wish your mother were here. I do. I wish your mother were here to see you like this. She would be so thrilled. Her little baby!" My grandma starts crying, and then Grandpa goes over and they bury their faces against each other. They are all hunched over together in the corner, and I'm standing here in my dress and my crown of flowers, just standing here, waiting.

On the way over in the car with Grandma driving, I am thinking it's weird. Being unrealistic and stupid one day, you change your name to Thumbelina and suddenly your life turns into the story. . . . The lights along Pottsboro Avenue are reflected in the puddles and raindrops on the windshield, giving everything a glittery exciting feeling, like I'm being whisked off to a faraway land in a storybook or something. Grandma looks over at me with a happy, proud face. Then a shade of worry crosses over her forehead and she says, "Louise, darling, do you really think the crown of flowers is appropriate for an art opening?"

"What?" I go. "Why not? It's a free country."

"Well, if you feel happy wearing it, then it's the right thing." And she looks over at me and says, "Oh, you are such a sketch!" My grandma always calls me "a sketch." This is an old word that none of my few friends have ever heard of. The Wizard of Oz, Snow White and the Seven Dwarfs, Sleeping Beauty. Thumbelina. The Ugly Duckling. Take your pick. We all adhere to one of those stories, even my grandma. And her vocab is just part of all that.

I lean my head against the car seat, and my feet do not touch the floor. I can see my patent leather shoes swinging there with those little white bows on the toes. Today I was with my grandma coming back from the grocery and some old geezer from one of her classes met us on the street and looked at me and said, "Oh, you must know my great-grandson over at Pottsboro Elementary. Are you a fourth grader too?" Later, Grandma tried to ease my pain by saying, "Oh, he's an idiot. Really, honey. He's always asking me if I get the 'special seniors over eighty-five' discount at the Bargain House."

Grandma switches on the radio to a rock station. To please me, I think, she turns up the volume. To be quite honest, I hate listening to loud music with my grandma.

Finally, Grandma stops the car before the Plow and Chaff Café. "Honey, have a *perfect* night," she says, and then another shade of worry draws across her face. She closes her eyes for a minute and then she blinks them open and smiles at me.

Chapter Twenty

I walk toward the lit-up café. It is completely jammed with people, tons of kids from North and even a few from South. I recognize some parents and a few aunts and uncles. I can see Annais's art teacher in there carrying an unlit pipe, wearing a beret, and chatting with Mrs. Elliot. I'm looking for Reni and Henderson. Where are they? I make my way to the refreshment table and there is Reni with an apron over her pink dress. She's handing out lemonade punch. I go and stand behind the table with her. "Hey ho, Thumbelina, Benny's going to love your dress," she says.

"Did you ask your mom about that room in the basement? Did she say I could live in it? I mean, nobody's using it, right?"

"I asked her. She said she's using it for laundry."

"Could I still move in there? I don't take up much room."

"My mom said maybe it's not a good idea," says Reni. "We'll think of something else. Okay?"

Some high school kids in one corner near us are drinking Pepsi. Annais is standing with them and I see her take a big drink and then start laughing. She is wearing an awesome all-beaded layered dress and really high heels, and she has dark eyeliner all around her eyes. She looks over at me, and her hands form plump fists at her side, and her eyes look suddenly blackened for a fight. "What?" I say to Reni.

Reni shrugs her shoulders and says, "Don't worry about it. Maybe she's just like that because all her teachers are here. Even Mr. Wagner."

"Oh, is that the teacher who loves that book *In the Road*?" I say.

"Yes," says Reni. "And did you see who's over there talking to him now?"

I look over at Mr. Wagner, and there is Benny McCartney. He's wearing a white shirt and a necktie and he has the book *On the Road* in his arms. He's kind of cradling it as he talks to the teacher. "*On the Road,*" I whisper to myself. "On. On. On. Not *in*. Okay?"

Annais swishes past the refreshment table and goes over to Mr. Wagner too, and the three of them start laughing.

Reni looks at me and goes, "What?"

"The pizza stalker looks nice in a necktie," I say. At the same time I am saying that, I am feeling confused and mixed up. I keep watching Mr. Wagner and Benny and Annais. I didn't realize Annais knew Benny. I mean, I didn't think that they were in the same class.

From across the room, I can see crazy Henderson up on a ladder. I look over at him, and for some dumb reason, the song "Frosty the Snowman" comes into my head. *Frosty the Snowman was alive as you and me. . . .* Henderson is going to be working the spotlights that will shine on the space at the microphone. He's way up on the top of the ladder and he's goofing off up there, acting like he's going to fall, throwing his arms around and making silly faces. Then he waves to me. "Thumb!" he calls. And he smiles at me. He pulls a piece of paper out of his pocket and holds it up. It says in big letters, KEEP HONKING. I'M RELOADING.

I frown at Henderson and I turn away, hoping Benny didn't notice. Luckily, he's still talking with Mr. Wagner and Annais. Reni and I start drinking lemonade. We both drink about five glasses. I mean, what else are you supposed to do at an art opening?

Suddenly, Benny is standing at the lemonade table. He's right in front of me, holding out a cup. Reni elbows me. "Go on," she says, "fill his cup. Thank him for the book."

"Hey," I go. "Thank you. I mean, thanks. Remember me, um, double cheese, double pepperoni, no onions?"

Benny smiles. "What, another customer of mine? This opening is full of my customers. You gotta forgive me; up here, I'm a big blur. Hey, I recognize her, though," he says, pointing to Reni. "You're Annais's sister, right? Bumper sticker, right?" Reni looks sheepish and doesn't answer. "I can't remember faces," he goes. "But jog my memory."

"Fan club?? Biggest fan? Uh, South Pottsboro Avenue," I say. "Third floor. Elevator building."

"Oh, yeah. Duh. You're the one who eats all that pizza. You order more pizza than Phi Sigma Delta over at Whitner. I'm not kidding. No offense, but for a little kid, that's a lot of tomato sauce."

"Oh," I say.

"Don't stop, though. It's good. Pizza's good stuff. Good for you. Lots of vitamins." Then he stops and looks at me for a minute. "Oh yeah, now I'm remembering something else. My mother helped you one day last year. That green house on Cinnamon Street. My mother helped you. I was outside in the yard too. My mother did her best. Really. She felt really bad. Ever since then, it's been empty, huh?"

"No, no, I don't remember. I really don't think that was me. No. It wasn't. No. No. It wasn't, not at all. No. Someone else. It was someone else."

"Oh," he goes, "well, then, sorry. Open mouth. Insert foot. Hey, is there any available lemonade or is this just, like, for display?"

"Oh, no, um, here," I say, lifting the pitcher and trying to pour. My wrist feels useless and my heart has become a terrible boom box with cranked-up volume, blaring away in my rib cage. "Reni, can you do this for me?" I lean against the table. Reni pours the glass, and Benny carries the lemonade back over to Mr. Wagner.

I feel like someone just hit me over the head with a hammer. The kind Dr. Birpkin uses to test my reflexes. It's a stupid bouncy little hammer that does absolutely nothing. Once he dropped it on the floor and it started bouncing around like crazy, like a little wild animal. But I feel like that hammer is inside my head now, pounding away, and I think to myself that I am not going to cry. In my mind I reach for my book, *Thumbelina: A Fairy Tale*. I turn the pages. I see the fat mole wearing a bow tie, the noisy rat in the tall reeds, the angry flock of crows circling above, the poor pink-breasted bird in the tunnel, lying as if dead in the soft gray dust. My head spins. I begin to drink lemonade. One glass after another.

Mr. Elliot comes by to get some lemonade. He looks at me and Reni, and I'm thinking to myself, "Don't say it." But he does. "Abbott and Costello!" he goes. "Having fun?"

"Oh, Thumbelina, I'm sorry," whispers Reni. "I'm really sorry. I got it wrong. It was my fault. It was my mistake. I was so sure."

Mrs. Elliot brushes by us, saying, "I'm going to start now, Guy." Guy is Mr. Elliot's first name. Guy is a nice guy. Ha ha. I'm not going to cry. No reason to cry. Guy won't cry, so why should I? Mr. Elliot signals to Henderson, who switches on the spotlight, and Mrs. Elliot walks over and holds her arms up at the audience in front of her like a politician. "Good evening, everyone!" The crowd cheers. "This is YOUR celebration as much as it is Annais's. This is about each and every one of YOU."

Someone shouts out, "Love you, Mrs. Elliot!"

"I'm going to start by saying that I want to encourage anyone who wants to come up here and talk about this show and my daughter Annais. You may have a poem about her work, you may want to comment, and I encourage this kind of involvement. I, for one, have watched Annais develop over the years. I have seen her talents coming to fruition. Can we give a round of applause for my Annais Elliot? I want to introduce my whole family to you now. Will my other daughter come up and my husband, and my son is over there doing the lights. As a family, we'd like to say thank you all for coming tonight." I look up at Mrs. Elliot as she hugs Annais. Reni is up there standing next to Mr. Elliot. Henderson just waves from his ladder perch. Someone takes a photo of The Elliot Family.

I stand back here with both hands flat on the table. Mrs. Elliot did not invite me to come up as one of her daughters, even though I helped with the show. Even though I'm there all the time. Even though I am sure I was born into that family. She must have forgotten. I must have slipped her mind for a moment.

Mrs. Elliot waves to the crowd like a president's wife and then walks away from the microphone, her family following her. The crowd cheers again. I look at Reni and she raises her eyebrows at me and tries to send me some kind of wordless Reni message.

"Reni," I whisper when she gets back to the table,

"your mom didn't mention me. She forgot to mention me. I'm like a daughter too, aren't I?"

Reni looks down at her lemonade. "Course you are," she says. "Don't feel bad about Benny. That was my fault."

For some dumb reason, I feel shaky and like I need to sit down. There are so many people in here and I forgot to eat anything before I left the condo. It feels like my eyes have tears in them. I take my hand and brush at my eyes and then I think I might have smeared my eye makeup. I pick up a napkin and start dabbing away at my eyes, but a stream of water keeps coming. Reni hands me a glass of lemonade and I gulp the whole thing. Then I knock over Reni's glass by mistake and lemonade spills all over my dress. I try to wipe up the lemonade, but I can feel the cold wetness seeping and spreading against my body.

Some kid from South goes up to the microphone and says, "Hey, I've been going over to the Elliots' house for, like, two years and I love Annais's paintings." The crowd laughs and the kid struts back and forth in the spotlight for a minute. But then he can't think of anything else to say. He just stands there looking stunned and pleased, basking in the glow of the spotlight.

Mr. Prigget, an art teacher from North, goes up and takes the microphone and says, "As you can imagine, I'm very proud indeed of Annais's paintings. I remember when she first came into my class and how much she's changed since then. By the way, I'd like to mention that I'm having a show at the Pottsboro Watercolor Club, and all are invited next Friday. For some, it's required. Six p.m. Friday, and if the *Pottsboro Shopping Guide* people are here for a review, you are also welcome to my show. Thank you."

Mrs. Cameron, an English teacher at North, comes up to the front of the audience and says, "Poets? Where are my poets? Anyone from 208 want to read one of their poems?"

"I do, Mrs. Cameron," says a girl with a blond ponytail. She comes up to the microphone and reads a poem about the end of summer and birds flying south. The poem has absolutely nothing to do with the paintings or Annais, but everyone applauds, and one of her friends calls out, "Go for it, Sandy Rolly!"

Then I see Benny McCartney moving up through the crowd. For a second, I think he is coming back toward the lemonade table, and my heart starts pounding and I feel dizzy, like I just did too many aerial cartwheels too fast, but he swerves and moves toward the microphone. I kind of lean against Reni. Henderson puts a weird green filter on the spotlight, so as Benny steps before the microphone, he has a green sickly cast to his face. I make an attempt to glare at Henderson, but I figure I'm lost in the darkened crowd. Benny stands there, and for a moment he sort of laughs and looks at the audience. Somebody shouts out, "Hey, Benny, make that a double cheese with anchovies."

Benny laughs again with the crowd. And then he clears his throat and says, "Annais." And then he holds up *On the Road* and shakes it in the air. Annais starts laughing. And Mr. Wagner starts clapping in a big exaggerated way to get everybody else started. Soon the whole room is clapping, and my cheeks are getting hot and I feel like maybe dizzy or off balance or something. Then Benny says, "I learned from reading *On the Road*, and from Mr. Wagner, that taking risks is sometimes optional but always admirable. So. Okay, here's my poem." He takes a deep breath and then he begins.

> *"Annais, the name is like a flock of geese,*
> *A flock of geese in a sky of blue.*
> *I know you sent the note,*
> *I hoped it was you.*
> *I was already yours, strong, sure, and true.*
> *Thanks for the bumper sticker.*
> *Thanks, love and peace,*
> *Annais, Annais, your name is like a flock of geese."*

The whole room seems to swoon, to rise like a great swollen wave, like a wave on Lake Mescopi when the police boat came through in the rain to ask my mother why we were sitting there with water in our boat. Everyone goes, "Ooooooh!" and then they start cheering again. The noise pounds in my ears.

Annais turns toward me for a split second and she laughs and throws her hands up in the air. Then she walks over and smiles at Benny and he takes her hand and smiles back at her. Everyone starts clapping again.

Suddenly, I feel like I can't breathe. The air is going into my mouth and then it won't go down any farther. I push past Reni and knock over a pitcher of lemonade. I stumble through the noisy crowd and scramble for the door. My head is spinning and I'm afraid I am going to fall or faint or throw up.

Finally, I get outside. It's raining even harder now. I run down the street. Cars rush past me, blowing rain all over my skirt and legs. I run through a muddy, cold puddle, and water pours into my shoes. *My mom is sitting in the rowboat. Her shoes are resting in the pool of water in the bottom of the boat.* A truck swishes past and street water splashes all over me, even hitting my face. My crown of flowers falls off into the darkness. I hear it land in the gutter. I hear the gutters roaring with water, screaming with rain, like deep inside the town, the hollow underground pipes are crying. The rain echoes above me and below me and around me. Everything is drowning and being sucked away into the drain, and the water keeps battering away at me, at the street, at the sidewalks, and I keep running.

Chapter Twenty-one

When I get to Cinnamon Street, I break one of the panes of glass in the back door and then I reach in and I unlock the door and turn the knob. I throw myself down on the living room floor. *My mom is sitting in the rowboat. There is water all over her shoes. I am sitting with her and I know. I know what she is going to do. I call out, "Mommy, don't. Please, please don't." It's because of my father. It's because he left us. He went away to New York to be with other people. Strangers to us. He forgot he was married to my mother. When you get married, it should be forever and ever and ever and ever, like the ceremony says. A father should not go away and leave his real wife and real daughter in a rowboat in the rain on Lake Mescopi.*

I want my mom. I want her back. Now. I need her now. I want back the way she tucked me in bed at night. I want the way she held me when she sang "Oh Stars in the Sky." I can remember her singing. I was looking out at the sky. I saw the great huge blackness of the night and the little lights of hope everywhere. I thought that feeling would stay with me forever, that my mom would rock me and sing to me forever and ever and ever.

Why does everybody in the world get what they want except me? Why does Merit Madson get what she wants? Why does Annais get what she wants? Why do Grandma and Grandpa and Reni and even Henderson, why do they all get what they want? Why can't I even have a mom and a dad and a house and a school I want? Other kids have that. Lots of kids, probably millions of them. Why can't I? Why can't I be tall? Why did all that have to happen? Why was it Benny McCartney who was there that day, of all the people in the world?

My mom and dad used to take me to gymnastics meets. My dad loved it. My mom made cookies for the refreshment stand. When I went to see my dad in New York City, he didn't even ask me one thing about gymnastics. He didn't ask if I finally got the double back handspring back tuck down. I could have done round off handsprings across his big beautiful honeymoon suite apartment, but he didn't even ask.

I look at her bedroom door. I do not want to open that door. No, I don't want to remember my mom lying there. I was screaming. I screamed and screamed, and a neighbor heard me and came to see what was wrong. I ran outside and I climbed that big tree. I went up there into the top branches. I climbed so high I could see all the world from there. There was a dark red sunset all smeared across the sky. I hid up there in the tree when the ambulance came. I saw them go into the house. I saw them take my mom away on a stretcher. She didn't move when they carried her out of the house.

I hid up there until night, when I saw all the stars and lights of the city and it was cold and my arms ached. I held on to the tree, but I was shivering and shaking and people were calling for me. They called Louise, Louise, Louise. I heard them but I didn't answer.

Finally, Grandpa got there and he heard me crying. He climbed up into the tree. They had ladders and lights and sirens, but Grandpa climbed up on his own for me and when he saw me, he said, "Oh, Louise, let me hold you. Let me hold you." And I let him hold me way high up in that big dark gnarled tree. I never knew grandpas cried. I never saw a grandpa cry before. He cried like a kindergartner.

And then he carried me down out of the tree. He carried me past all the men in firemen's hats, past flashing lights and lines of people. My grandpa carried me to his car and we drove away. And as we were driving, I fell asleep, and while I was sleeping, I was kind of forgetting everything. Everything. Everything. Everything. But not really. No, not really.

I stand up now and turn around the room. The light from the streetlamps comes through the curtains as I move toward the shut bedroom door. I take the door handle and turn it and walk in. The bedroom is empty. There is nothing in there at all. The streetlight falls through the window. I go to sit on the floor where the edge of the bed used to be.

The cars on the street swish by. Their lights run up the walls and drop away, making strange patterns on the floor and on my arms in the darkness. I am never leaving this house. I'm not going back to that art opening. Mrs. Elliot is not my mother. Mr. Elliot is not my father. This is my mother. This. Here. She wanted freedom from her life. This is what she wanted. I sit on the floor and cry until I have cried more tears than the rain falling outside.

After a while, I hear a noise in the house. Footsteps brush across the floor. And I look up and see a large shadow in the doorway. I look up, but I cannot tell who is there, and then another car swishes by outside and lights up the walls and I see it's Henderson. He sits down on the floor beside me and he puts his arm around me and I lean on his flannel shoulder. For a long time we don't speak at all.

Finally I say, "My mother killed herself. She died in this room here. Benny McCartney's mother was walking by outside. She heard me screaming. She came to help. She called the ambulance." Henderson lets me sob against his shoulder, all the while cars flash by outside and their lights ride up and down the lace curtains at the windows. The lights slide across the room and then retreat. They roll over our faces as we sit on the dark floor on Cinnamon Street.

"Everybody hates me. Annais hates me. Benny hates me. And Merit Madson and Janie Brevette hate me. They hate me because I'm small. Because I look like a grade school kid. Because I won't grow and I'm just not cool and grown-up-looking and because I don't have a mother and a father. That's why they hate me. That's why they wanted me off the gymnastics team. Because I'm so small and stupid-looking and because I have no parents," I say.

"No, Thumb. That's not why," says Henderson. "Don't you know why?"

"No," I say.

"They wanted you off the team because they are *jealous* of you. You're too good at gymnastics. When I first saw you, I couldn't believe how graceful and quick you were. And you're beautiful. You are beautiful, Thumb."

"No," I say. "I'm not."

"Yes," says Henderson. "You are beautiful. Don't you think I would know?"

"I am?" I say and I look back at Henderson, and his face in the light from the streetlamp is softly pale and glowing. "Are you sure?"

"Yes," he says.

I push my head into his shoulder. "Oh, Henderson, you're such a good friend. The best friend I have ever had." Henderson leans his head on top of my head and keeps his arms around me.

• • •

I can't remember how long we stay there, but finally we walk back to the party in the darkness, the trees above us full of wind and blowing rain. The streets and sidewalks are strewn with shattered twigs and leaves and tiny pieces of broken things that somehow got pulled apart by the rain and wind.

The opening is mostly over when we get there. Thank goodness. My grandma is sitting in the car, waiting for me, and she beeps the horn from the parking lot across the way and waves. I button up my jacket and head across the shiny wet street. "Henderson, thank you," I call.

And he calls back, "Thumbelina?"

And I go, "What?" And he just stands there and doesn't say anything.

My grandma drives the car to South Pottsboro in silence. She doesn't try to impress me with any loud rock music. She doesn't try to ask me about what happened. She seems somehow to know. How does my grandma know everything? It's weird. I just sit there quietly beside her and we put the heater on high to help dry out my soaking shoes and my ice-cold dress.

When I get home, my grandpa says, "How's our party girl?" And then his face falls, collapses into millions of pieces, the way everything seemed to crumble and disintegrate in that movie *Thelma and Louise*. I go in my room and close the door.

I am still shivering and I feel like I have a sore throat. My forehead feels hot. I unbutton my wet jacket. I am feeling very feverish. I have chills and I lie down and pull a cover over me, still wearing my wet dress. Next to me on the pillow is my favorite book in the whole world. I have read it every night since I got it. *Thumbelina: A Fairy Tale*. I pick it up and look at the beautiful cover. And then I remember Henderson holding me in the shadowy room on Cinnamon Street, the soft brush of his flannel shirt, his sad steady eyes. In a haze of fever, I say out loud, "Benny didn't send me this book. Henderson sent it."

Chapter Twenty-two

Sometime in the middle of the night, I become aware that I am sick. My throat is burning and my ears are ringing. I get up to go to the bathroom and I start shaking with chills. Grandma sees me from her bedroom and calls out, "Louise, are you all right?" I stumble and fall on the floor and Grandma gets out of bed and comes over to me.

The room feels like a wobbling spaceship lost somewhere in the dark sky. "Louise, Louise," she says, "drink this water and take this Tylenol. Lift your head up."

Somehow I am back in my bed and there is light coming through my penguin curtains. For some reason the bills on the penguins are the brightest yellow I've ever seen. One of the penguins seems to be waddling as the curtain quivers in the draft. Has it stopped raining? I have a glass of water right near my face. I don't think I can sit up to drink it.

Then it's night again and my pillow is damp and when I open my eyes, my grandma is leaning over my bed. She has a tray of food in her arms. "Louise," she says, "you haven't eaten anything for two days. I have some soup for you. Do you want to try eating some?"

"No. No. I can't."

Now the penguins are in shadows. Their faces are dark and gloomy-looking. The baby penguin has fallen over. Grandma turns on a light and it hurts my eyes. She fluffs a pillow behind my head, I think, and she offers me a sip of soup on a spoon. I tilt my head and take it. "What time is it?" I ask, and Grandma says it's afternoon. "Which afternoon?" I ask.

I sleep and sleep and sleep and my dreams are confusing. I am moving through layers of penguin curtains. I get lost in the blowing light fabric. My mother takes my hand and leads me through them. She tells me something very important. She whispers it in my ear. It rolls over me like a breeze from the open window. When I wake up, I remember that she told me something important that day in the rowboat. I remember what she said.

When I open my eyes, I see a bouquet of lilacs by my bed. Grandpa is sitting near me, reading. The window is open a crack and the curtains are breathing in and out in the air. Then I fall back asleep and days go by, or weeks, I don't really know. I keep sleeping and sleeping.

Sometime, somewhere, I wake up again and Grandma sits on the edge of my bed. I think it is afternoon. I keep my head on the pillow and I tell her what happened at the opening and what happened after. I tell her how I went to Cinnamon Street and broke in. "Grandma, we need to fix the back door window now. Tell Grandpa," I say. Then I tell her what I remember.

All of it. I even tell her about my mom and the way I had found her that day lying in her bed. I tell her about the tree and me way high up in the arms of it screaming. I tell her everything, and then Grandma and I fall against each other, our foreheads touching. My grandma's tears fall on my cheeks and my tears fall on hers. "Isn't it strange that it was Benny's mother who came in the house? She called the ambulance," I say.

"It was Benny who touched off your memory, honey. Yes, it was. He helped you remember," says my grandma.

"I miss her," I say. "It hurts so much."

"Me too, honey. Me too. But it's a terrible thing to bury something inside you and never let it out. It's better to face it, to yell and to scream and to cry and let it out. For both of us. Good not to keep things bottled up, because when you bottle things up, they can go off like a volcano."

"I think I did go off like a volcano, Grandma, just like the one in the state of Washington," I say. "And now it hurts because I miss her and I remember her. I didn't want to remember her."

"Oh, honey. Honey. Honey," Grandma says, hugging me. "Oh, honey, honey, honey, honey, honey, honey, honey."

·   ·   ·

My grandma draws back the penguin curtains for the first time in maybe a week. A week and a half? She opens the window and I can see that outside, it is spring finally. There are little green leaves on the trees and there is the sound of tiny unseen birds singing. There is a thick warmth to the air and a sort of pale yellow cast to everything. The lilacs in the vase by my bed fill the room with a delicate spring smell. "Your grandpa picked these for you," says Grandma.

"Tell him thanks," I say. "They're beautiful." And I close my eyes again and drift away into sleep, but it isn't a confusing, terrible, dark sleep anymore, it's a gentle resting kind of sleep.

Chapter Twenty-three

When you are sick, you think of all kinds of very dumb things. One of the things that floats into my mind is that new T-shirt shop that opened up in the South Pottsboro shopping mall a while ago. The owner has been offering to make T-shirts with anything you want written on them for only five dollars a shirt. Suddenly, everyone in South Pottsboro has been wearing shirts with things written on them, things that are hard to say out loud and easier to put in writing. Grandma and I saw this guy and girl in a restaurant, and the guy's T-shirt said, DARLA, WILL YOU MARRY ME?

"Isn't that a hoot!" my grandma said. "Now, how did he do that?"

I explained it to my grandma and she went, "Aha, I get it. Maybe I should have a T-shirt printed that says, 'Phil, it's time to turn off the TV, put it in its suitcase, and go to sleep.'"

"Oh, Grandma," I say.

I get out of bed and I go to the window. There is a pink magnolia tree in bloom right in front of our building. It's so beautiful and I never even noticed it before. "Oh, that tree," says my grandpa when he brings me some more soup, "that tree is why we bought this place. I mean it's the most beautiful tree in the whole world." Grandpa sets the tray down. I look up at him, and his face is framed by an explosion of pink and red magnolia flowers behind him out the window. In my mind I have a T-shirt made. It says, "Love you, Grandpa. Love you. Love you. Love you. Love you."

The veggie noodle soup is like magic. It's my grandma's secret Wizard of Oz potion. I eat it all and then I lean back on my pillow and check my cell phone. I see that Reni has been leaving messages, worrying about me, wondering where I am. But there's nothing from Henderson.

I walk around my room, and it feels seriously good to be out of bed and on my feet again. I think I've been sick for more than a week. It feels like forever.

When I try to call Henderson, a message comes on immediately that says, "Hey, the robots from planet Zing Zong have zapped Henderson Elliot to a distant galaxy. Please leave a message."

Later in the afternoon, when I'm lying on top of my covers, basically better but not all better, Grandma taps on my door. "Sweetie," she calls, "you have a visitor. Reni is here. Reni. Reni. Reni." Grandma has her arms around Reni when she opens the door. My grandma is so glad to see Reni, it's as if saying her name once isn't enough. She has to repeat the name three times because once doesn't say it all. My grandma knows that Reni is huggable and lovable, but Reni doesn't know it and there's no way to make her know something like that. She has to find out for herself.

"Reni Reni Reni!" I go.

And Reni says, "Thumbelina. Thumbelina. Thumbelina."

And Grandma goes, "Oh, you gals don't miss a beat, do you?"

Reni's carrying a bouquet of roses. "A lady at a flower shop gave me these. They were free," she says, "because they're on their last legs."

"Oh, like me," I go. "Ha ha."

Reni sits on my bed with the fading roses in her arms. She looks at me. Then she squeezes her eyes real tight and frowns. Finally she says, "I'm a jerk for mixing you up with Benny M. No, it was my fault. I led you astray. It wasn't you. Are you okay?"

"Yes. No. I don't know," I say. "I'm okay. But I remembered everything about my mom. You know? You know what I mean. So be careful. I might start crying. Do you think you can be friends with a true Kleenex hound?"

"It was my fault. I'm the serious jerk," goes Reni. "I went wild and ate two tubs of ice cream and a whole box of cookies and four ham sandwiches. I've gained five pounds this week. I'm sooo bummed. It's too late now. I'll never get to go to the Spring Fling Dance."

"Me neither, Reni. But it's only one dance, and there will be others coming along. My grandma says there will be lots more dances. And we're gonna change things. Soon, everybody in the world will be begging to be our friends. Come on, Reni, put 'em up. Put 'em up." I make two small fists and I hold them in front of my face.

Reni looks down at the roses. "Even if I had lost twenty pounds, Justin Bieber wouldn't show up from Hollywood to take me to the Spring Fling Dance. He never even answered my letters."

"No," I say, "probably not. Hey, letters only cause trouble."

"Yeah," goes Reni, "maybe. Still, if Henderson hadn't been gone, I wouldn't have eaten that whole tub of macaroni and cheese at midnight. Henderson guards over the fridge. He would have stopped me."

"He would have?" I say. "Henderson stops you from eating stuff?"

"Yeah," she goes.

"Where is Henderson anyway? He doesn't answer his cell."

"He got accepted at the writer's camp in Idaho. He'll be there for a few more weeks. He can't have a cell phone there. It's against camp rules. But he can call home once a week from their office," says Reni. "This is a big deal, you know."

"Has he called home yet?" I say.

"Yeah," goes Reni, "he's having a pretty good time. They have an indoor pool there. He's written fifteen more pages on his novel. He's changed the title and there's some girl who's in love with him. She's been following him around, calling him a genius."

"She's stalking him!" I say "He should notify the authorities immediately."

"No," says Reni. "He didn't say she was stalking him."

"Oh," I say and look down at my fingernails that I painted with silver nail polish the night of the party. When I'd finished painting them, Grandpa said, "Looks like you just slammed your fingers in a car door, pal." Maybe so. Maybe so. (I am chairman of the board of idiots who don't know until it's too late what they feel.) I need to talk to Henderson. Who is this creep following him everywhere, throwing around words writers love to hear? I mean, tell a writer he's a genius and of course he'll start liking you. But that's cheating. I have to talk to Henderson. It can't wait.

"When are you going back to school?" says Reni. One of the roses on her lap is dropping its petals. They fall on the floor around her feet.

"Soon," I say.

"Good, I'm glad you're going back. I was worried about you."

"Thanks," I say.

"Thumbelina?" says Reni. "If Benny didn't write the note and if Benny didn't send you the book, then who did?'"

I look at Reni and I get tears in my eyes again. I remember Henderson holding me in the darkness of Cinnamon Street. I remember his long arms around me. I remember his voice softly in my ear. *"Frosty the snowman was alive as you and me."* I take Reni's hand and I squeeze it and I don't say anything. I keep looking at Reni and tears keep rolling and pouring out of my eyes.

Then Reni's cell phone rings and it's her mom. She wants Reni to go to Tall Girl with Annais while she buys her some spring clothes. "My mom says I have to go along to show support and give my opinion."

"Reni, tell me something. Does Annais *ever* have to show support to you?" I say.

"Oh, wow, look at the tree outside your window. It looks like a big bouquet from heaven," says Reni.

"Yeah," I say. "Anyway, I hate going to Tall Girl. I always feel like such a small girl. But do they have a shop called Small Girl? No."

"Duh," goes Reni, and she stands up to leave. "These roses need to be in water." She smiles. She looks five pounds fatter and five pounds sadder.

"Reni," I say to her, "oh, Reni." I want to throw my arms around her. I want to call up Justin Bieber and beg him to write to her. But I can't and I won't. "Oh, Reni," I say. "Oh, Reni. Reni. Reni."

Chapter Twenty-four

In the next couple of days, lots of memories of my mom begin coming back to me. It's so strange. Sometimes I'll text Reni about one of them. I'll go, "Reni, I remember ice-skating with my mom. It was so cool."

And Reni will text back, "Sick. You know how to ice-skate?"

Other times I'll even text my grandpa. He loves that. He's a whiz at texting. I'll go, "Grandpa, I remember my mom taking me to school on my very first day of kindergarten."

And he'll text back, "Luv you."

I do remember that first day at school. I was afraid to get in line with the others. There were so many kids. Everyone was bigger than me. My mom cried in a quiet way and then she said, "Go on, little penguin. Little penguin. I'll be here at two thirty to pick you up." Those steps across the playground were scary. The school building was enormous. The other children were so strong and noisy. Halfway there, I turned around to wave good-bye and saw my mother standing far away in the distance across the field of grass by the school yard. She was waving to me.

I could never be mad at my mother for what she did on Cinnamon Street. When it first happened and I had forgotten everything, counselors at school used to say to me, "Aren't you angry at your mother for what she did?" And I would not understand. Angry? Mad? All I have to do now is think of her at the edge of that blowing green grass, standing there all by herself, waving to me. How small and cloudy she became. I knew then that I would lose her. I always knew I would lose her.

My grandma has been saying, "Some people are

just not meant to be in this world. It's just too much for them. Your mother was one of those people." Believe it or not, it feels better to remember, even though it hurts, and sometimes when I'm alone in my room, I cry. And more memories come back to me and in some funny way, I feel I carry them around with me, as if my mom is a part of me now. Would Reni think this is psychotic of me? Henderson would understand. He would. I *know* he would.

Suddenly, I decide to get dressed and go up on the roof. My grandma says, "Honey, if you get up too early, you can have a relapse. Be easy on yourself. You're mending."

I have this image suddenly of me as a rag doll with all these mends all over my body. There's a mend even over my heart. I think about my mother again. I reach out and take her hand in my mine. Seriously, *is* this psychotic of me? I want my mom. I want her back. I need her now. She walks with me toward the door. I feel her hand in mine.

I turn around and look at my grandma. "Can we call up those four goons who carried off my balance beam and tell them to bring it back?" I say.

My grandma looks at me, and her face kind of melts into pure breathtaking, dazzling relief.

I climb the stairs to the sky. Stepping out into the sunlight, the whole world is in bloom. It's like while I slept, everything was changing. I can see lilac bushes and apple trees all over South Pottsboro, and every one of them is covered in flowers. For some reason this makes my eyes tear up again.

Mr. Anderson is up here planting his vegetable roof garden with twelve watermelon plants under plastic bubbles. I sit down on a chair in the sun and I nod to Mr. Anderson. He's wearing green Farmer Jones type overalls and a farmer's straw hat. "Louise, he's a retired banker who always wanted to be a farmer," my grandma said to me earlier. "Isn't it wonderful! And even better, we all get free watermelons in late summer. That wasn't in the condo documents!"

The sun feels sooo nice on my legs. I'm kind of thinking again about that letter Coach Tull wrote. I'm also thinking about what Henderson said about Merit Madson and Janie Brevette. Henderson is pretty smart. I suppose he could be right. If he's right and they're just jealous, then that's not so bad.

While I've been sitting here, Mr. Anderson has set out all these little green, tender new watermelon plants. They look so eager somehow, all lined up in a row in the soil, like it's their time now finally after millions and billions of years. It's their moment on the roof. Wow. I wish I could tell Henderson that. I think he's the only person in the world who wouldn't go, "Huh?" when I said that. But now he's gone away to writer's camp and I can't tell him anything. I feel like I've been wandering around lost in the snowy woods, completely baffled about what I feel. It was all buried under snow. I think then about the book Henderson sent me. *Thumbelina: A Fairy Tale.* The person who sent me that book knows me all the way down to my toes. And it's Henderson.

Suddenly, I want to have one of those T-shirts made. It will say across the front in big letters, HEN, CAN YOU EVER FORGIVE ME FOR BEING SUCH AN IDIOT? I MISS YOU SO MUCH.

Chapter Twenty-five

Right now I'm headed for South Middle and I do feel a little bit weak. It happens when you stay in bed for more than a week. Good thing I'm not trying to learn English. Go explain *weak* and *week* to a foreign exchange student. The first thing I'm planning to do is see Coach Tull. I just want to talk to him quietly. No big deal. I'm running, so that's why there are tears in my eyes, again. For someone who's hardly ever cried before, this month has been a revisiting time for me and my tear ducts. They have become overactive.

I'm thinking too about my balance beam. In my mind I'm at that yard sale and I'm saying to those four high school dorks that are carrying it off, "Wait a freaking minute. Put my freaking balance beam down. Put it down. It's not for sale. Back off. Don't touch that beam. It's mine. It's me and I don't want to sell it." Since I was sick and got better, I'm like Miss Healthy from planet Get Out Of My Face. I'm like Miss Sure-Foot from planet Take No Flack. Hello, Merit Madson. I'm on my way. I'm coming back. Are you ready to be reported for your terrible deeds?

That balance beam was the last present from my mom and my dad. The last thing they ever did together was to go to that factory and look at small balance beams for me. They went together. I wasn't there, but I can imagine how it must have been. My mom may have had her arm locked in my dad's as they walked toward the factory. She was smiling at him. She loved him so much. And there was something unspoken and important between them, and that something was me. Me on the gymnastic mat, bounding into a string of front walkovers or aerial cartwheels or standing upside down in a quiet handstand, balancing on my palms and fingers while my legs did a careful, planned, and ordered dance above me.

When I came home that day, there were ribbons tied around both ends of the beam, and a helium balloon attached to the middle that said, *Happy Birthday, Louise!* A balance beam is one of the heaviest things in the world. Henderson says that when you are on certain planets in outer space, the gravity is so strong that most people while visiting there would weigh thousands of pounds. I wonder what my balance beam would weigh on Jupiter or Mars. Millions and trillions of pounds? I can't believe my parents went to that huge effort to buy me an enormous heavy balance beam and then, after all that, my dad could walk away and marry somebody else and have some other little girl call him Daddy.

I walk past all the kids on the steps at school. They're in their little cliques. I know those circles and how they seal over, leaving no room to beg, steal, or borrow for an entrance. I know. Believe it or not, I want no entrance. In my mind I'm on the balance beam, walking carefully among them, looking for my reference point, each measured step bringing me closer to the moment when I will throw my body up into the air and then curl down into a tight spinning tuck and land squarely back on my two steady, reliable feet.

I push through the double doors and walk downstairs toward Coach Tull's office. When I get there, I knock once and open the door.

Coach Tull is sitting at his desk with all this sports equipment piled around him. He's got a basketball next to his computer, a pile of red and green heavy rings scattered across his desk, like a child in a playpen with his toys around him. "Louise Terrace!" he says, drinking coffee from a scratched-up old jar. Coach T always drinks coffee from the same glass canning jar, and he used to put on blues music really loud while we practiced. He loves the blues. And he used to cook us all Chinese food on Tuesday night at his house. Seeing him there with his canning-jar coffee cup, everything comes back to me. "Whoa, what a surprise, Louise. What a surprise!"

I sit down beside his desk for a minute and I just look at my hands in my lap and say absolutely nothing for a minute. I'm afraid if I say one word, I will cry. "Louise, I'm so glad to see you. You can't know how glad I am. To what do we owe the pleasure after all this time?" he says. I don't answer. Then he says, "The team has not been the same since you left. You know that."

"Thank you," I say. Then I hand him a large envelope full of Merit Madson's notes. "You can have a look at this in your spare time."

"Does this mean you're thinking of coming back?" he says, taking the large envelope and putting it on his desk. "I'm going to say that I would be very happy about that."

"Thank you for your letter," I finally say. "It helped. I have some things to tell you about some of the team members. It's in the envelope. But thanks again for that letter. It made all the difference."

"What letter?" says Coach Tull.

"The letter you wrote asking me to come in and talk to you. That's why I'm here."

"Louise, that's not our policy. We're not allowed to pressure students into sticking with a sport. We're not

201

allowed to write letters like that. The wish to be part of a team sport has to come from within the individual student. Not that I didn't want to urge you back. But I couldn't. You said you were bored with it. I took you at your word. I'll be honest; you're a wonderful gymnast, and with a little work, you could be looking at All State next year. Easy."

"Wait a minute," I say, looking at Coach Tull, at his fingers locked around his jar of coffee. "Wait a minute." The room is turning over like I'm in an aerial cartwheel with nowhere to land or some kind of miscalculated butterfly twist that has left me falling from the high beam into a net below that catches me in its soft, web-like grip.

"Wait a minute. You didn't write me a letter?"

"No," says Coach Tull again, "but I am so glad you're here."

Chapter Twenty-six

I am back in school and two weeks have gone by since I was sick. Spring is in full bloom now. The lilacs have come and are almost gone. They are my grandma's favorite, and Grandpa has been bringing her a bouquet every chance he gets. He holds each bouquet behind his back and every time he presents one to her, she squeals with delight and acts surprised and touched, and it has been a very mushy spring all the way around.

Reni has been coming over to my house a lot more, which I appreciate, because I have stopped going over to the Elliots' house altogether. I just don't need to be there anymore. In my mind when I say that, my mother squeezes my hand. I'm not a sicko or a psychopath; I don't mean she really does. It's like an inner something that I can feel all through me.

And something else happened recently. It involves yet another letter. One day we received a long white envelope from the public health department in East Pottsboro. Grandma was doing her yoga on the living room rug when Grandpa brought the letter up and opened it. Grandma happened to be upside down standing on her head at the time, which is why her face turned the darkest red and why she fell over with a soft thud as he read the letter.

Dear Mr. and Mrs. Terrace,

I am happy to inform you that the wrappings around your furnace pipes at 42 South Pottsboro Avenue have tested negative for asbestos. They are made of a certain wool fiber which looks similar but is not at all asbestos. I am pleased to be the bearer of good news.

> *Sincerely yours,*
> *Bill Britton*
> *Pottsboro Public Health Officer*
> *Department of Public Health*

"But it's not possible. I know what asbestos looks like," said Grandma.

Grandpa smiled. "Baby doll, stick with me. We're going places."

As a result of these findings, Grandpa has been saying, "I told you so," to everything. He's been strutting around like Mr. Big Mouth from planet All Ego. He's been doing more Tai Chi, hogging the living room, and he's not going to eat health food anymore. He's been cooking nonorganic chicken right under Grandma's nose and he's very happy about it. My grandma has been a bit more sedate these days, like a rabbit with her ears pinned back. She's never been wrong before.

If you hang out with my grandma, you discover soon enough she is seriously weird. I mean, she knows things that normal people don't. She'll go, "Honey, you are going to want this sweater later today. Take it with you to school. I know you'll need it." And I'll go, "No, Grandma, I'm not taking that thing. I'm fine." And then around two o'clock in the afternoon, I'm freezing my butt off, thinking, "Way to go, Grandma." How many times this spring did she say, "You know who I'm voting for? The youngster who you spend all your time with, the one you tell everything to, the one who looks at you with so much brightness. . . . Henderson? Henderson!" But that was back when I was lost under snow.

As for me, there have been some good things and some bad things. I cannot stop missing Henderson. I agree, it's totally weird but it's true. Every day I'm just waiting for him to come home. I hate that writers' camp and I hate that girl poet whose name turned out to be Agarina. I have to agree with Grandpa; some of these names are over the top. Agarina sounds like *aggravate*. I hope Henderson notices that.

Reni tells me that Henderson has been going on picnics with her after rap poetry class. She's been helping him edit his novel. No. No. I'm the one he reads to, not her. I can't explain anything to Reni. This she will not understand at all. She'll think I'm a lunatic. *I* think I'm a lunatic.

It took me a while to figure out who had written the letter from Coach Tull, since Coach Tull didn't write it. Whoever wrote it was brilliant and daring and stupid all at the same time. "Who could that possibly be?" I said to myself. Then I got out the brown wrapping paper that my Thumbelina book came in. I compared the handwriting of the address on the package with the signature of Coach Tull at the bottom of the letter. The *T* in *Terrace* and the *T* in *Tull* were identical and written by the same hand. My bestest best. My Henderson sent them both. He sent them both. The floor just fell out from under me.

I wish I could say that this incident helped ease these feelings that have been confusing me and baffling me lately. But it didn't help at all and only made things worse. Where Reni is concerned, I have become totally annoying, pestering her to death with questions about a brother she secretly wants to kill. Of course I can't tell her how I feel. She will have me arrested for insanity. She'll go, "Oh my gosh, you have truly gone over the edge, Thumbelina, just like Thelma and Louise."

It's a normal ho-hum evening. Grandpa is playing Trivial Pursuit, the sixties version, all by himself. My grandpa is a baby boomer. He went to Woodstock but got stuck in traffic that stretched for miles and never actually got in. He's an expert on the 1960s. He is asking the questions out loud now and then answering them himself, questions like How many rings did the Beatle Ringo Starr wear on May 15, 1965?

Then out of the blue, my grandma says, "Honey, we haven't measured you in a while. Let's see if you've grown." So I stand up against the wall, my heart beating inside me like a sorrowful drum all alone in the cave of my being. Will I ever grow up? Will I ever be big and tall? When I go back to the gymnastics team next fall and we do a team photo, will I be the medium-height girl smiling in the second row? Will I walk out one day into the world and know it is mine?

I lean my head back against the markings on the doorjamb, and my grandma slides a book across the top of my head. She marks the spot with a pencil and I stand away as she measures the mark.

"My goodness. You are exactly four feet seven and one-eighth inches. You've grown one-eighth of an inch! It's not much, but it's an indication, a good indication. I told you growing starts from the inside first, honey, and in that way, you've been growing like wildfire," my grandma says, beaming at me like a clear, bright star in a galaxy I am just discovering.

Chapter Twenty-seven

To be honest, there have been more letters in my life this month than I ever thought possible. Just when it seems the letters have come to an end, another one appears. This latest one is in Reni's hand when I open the condo door. There she is in the hall, bouncing off the walls. She smiles down at me like she's carrying a hidden jar of jelly beans. She's hopping on one foot and then on the other. "I got a letter, Thumbelina. I got a letter!" she says, waving her hands around. "A letter from Justin Bieber. It happened. It's a miracle!!"

Reni blows into the apartment like a gust of pink wind. Her face is blooming and radiant. She flies toward the couch and holds out the letter. "It came from Montana."

"Justin Bieber lives in Montana?" I say.

"Well," says Reni, "he's probably hiding out from overzealous fans there. He's probably camping out somewhere in the Rockies with a fake name to get a little peace and quiet."

"In the Rockies? That sounds spooky," I say.

"Read it, Thumbelina. Read the letter."

I take a deep breath and I look up at Reni. "Come on, Reni, I want to know. Which one are you, Abbott or Costello?" I ask her. She laughs and I hook my arm in hers and then I open her letter. I read:

Dear Reni Elliot,

Thank you so much for your passionate letters, all five of them. I thought they were very beautiful. I'm not in opposition to writing to fans when they are as delightful as you are. You seem like such a nice person and there aren't enough nice people in this world. Although I already have a girlfriend, I still hold your letters special to me. I hope you will not feel baffled by the amount of time it took me to write back. I have been very busy.

Sincerely yours,
Justin Bieber

" 'Sincerely yours, Justin Bieber.' Isn't it so cool. Isn't it the best letter in the world?" says Reni.

"Wow, Reni," I say. "This is outstanding. Finally. Finally he writes to you. This is wonderful."

There are some phrases in the letter like "I'm in opposition to" and "I hope you will not feel baffled by" that give me some thought. Some *serious* thought.

But all I say is "Reni, this proves it. It appears to be a fair world in spite of everything."

"Yup," says Reni, flopping her pink high-tops up on the coffee table. "Yup, it is. Really fair. And I've been so happy about this letter that I went and did something."

"What?" I say.

"I got up the nerve and went alone to the Diabetes Walkathon, and you'll never guess who I walked with the whole way."

"Who?" I say.

"Newton Mancini. He's a riot. He's got this little dog named Bill and he tells all these Bill stories."

"Reni, this is so cool," I say.

"Yeah," she goes, "and he asked me to help him sell sugar-free cookies at his booth at the Spring Fling and I accepted."

"You did?" I say.

"Yes, I did. I think I always liked that red pizza delivery jacket."

"So, *you're* the pizza stalker," I say.

"Yup," she goes. "I guess so."

"Nice, Reni," I say, "I'm proud of you. You know what? If you end up marrying Newton Mancini, your name will be Reni Mancini."

And then we both start roaring away because, when it comes to laughing, Reni and I are tops.

Chapter Twenty-eight

Oh, but still no word from Henderson. The space that Hen used to occupy is silent and far reaching. When the phone rings, he's the first thing I think of. And yes, this morning the phone is ringing. The windows are open and I can hear Henderson's dinosaurs chirping and singing outside in the flowering trees along the street. The phone keeps ringing and ringing. We have a few new electronic devices in our life now. Grandpa has purchased a telephone with a caller ID on it. Finally we can now see who's calling before we answer.

My grandma and I are sitting on the couch and we both look down at the phone number on the little screen. It's from New York City. It's my dad. Grandma and I look at each other and then she says, "Sweetie, let's not answer it. He just wants to buy the green house on Cinnamon Street for a good price. He wants a bargain. But I'm not selling it to him. I bought it for your mother. I paid for it. It's mine and I don't want to sell it to him. And I don't want to speak to him ever again."

"Me neither," I say. I feel a pang down in the distant edges of my heart. It's another tug that comes with more tears. So much water. I must be the polar ice caps melting. I must be the living proof of the greenhouse effect. *Me neither. I don't want to talk to him either.* The phone keeps ringing and ringing, like my dad's voice repeating, "Okay? Okay? Right? Okay?"

"No, not okay," I say to myself. "Not okay. Not okay. Not okay."

Grandpa comes in the room and he stops still and looks at the phone. For some dumb reason, that woman climber comes into my mind again. She would have been the first American woman to climb to the top of

Mount Everest. But instead she's frozen somewhere, lost in time. I went on Google this morning and I found out her name. It was Marty Hoey. She was lovely and young and brave when she fell off that mountain. "Grandpa," I say out of the blue, "how do you decide to name a bench in South Pottsboro?"

"Well," he says, "that's the town planning committee's job. That's my department."

"Could we name a bench after someone?" I say.

"Well, we can talk about that," he says.

"Good," I say, "because I want to have a Marty Hoey bench. I want her to be remembered. And I want one for my mother too. I want one for both of them."

The phone keeps ringing and ringing. Then Grandpa turns off the ringer and all we can see is my dad's phone number blinking on the little screen. Finally the number disappears.

Grandma smiles at me and says, "I'm not selling to him. Ever. But I was actually going to talk to you about selling the green house to someone else possibly. We have a private buyer."

"We do?" I say and I feel another tug, another pang pinging pinging inside me.

"Yes," says my grandma. "There's a family in North Pottsboro and, honey, they seem very nice."

"You want to sell it to them?" I say.

"Well, only if you want to. But it might be useful to have the money. Then we could buy something bigger for the three of us."

Grandpa looks at me very carefully, like I'm a complicated map he's trying to read in the car with only a flashlight.

"You know the lady downstairs?" says Grandma.

"Yes," I say. "The one who hates Grandpa." Grandpa tilts his head and raises his eyebrows and looks pleased.

"Yes," says my grandma, swirling around. She puts her elbow on Grandpa's shoulder and leans her head on her arm and smiles up close into Grandpa's face. "Yes, that lady hates hates hates your grandpa. Mean old Grandpa. BUT she absolutely *loves* me."

"She wants to sell her condo downstairs, pal, and your crazy grandma wants to buy it. Anyway, I don't know why that lady hates me. I always brought her mail up for her and I even walked her dog sometimes. But she's a space cadet and she got scared off by the asbestos thing your grandma dragged us into. I told you there would be problems, baby doll."

"Well, it's not a problem, dear. Her condo is wonderful. It's much better than this one. It's full of light, honey. It has two and half baths and a large living room and big kitchen, and there's even a room where someone could put a balance beam and floor mat for practice, if that someone wanted to."

Suddenly my grandma and grandpa come up and stand close around me, like we're in a football huddle. We push there, the three of us, in a tight circle. On both sides I can feel them standing by me.

I keep quiet for a minute, listening to the words pour over me now like warm rain. I think about the house on Cinnamon Street. I wrap my arms around it and hold it against me for a moment. I push my face against the walls and I rest my forehead along the roof. Then I open my arms, and like a dream, I let the house go. It floats out of my arms and away into the clouds, just like in *The Wizard of Oz*, and when that green house lands, it will belong to someone else and it will have another chance at life and a whole new start.

Chapter
Twenty-nine

At four thirty on Thursday, May 20, one month before
school lets out, Henderson comes home. "He arrived
on the train," Reni says to me on the phone. "He likes
to ride on trains cause he's a doofus. He says he looks
out the window as they are moving along and it releases
his unconscious so he can write. You know Henderson.
He has these geeky theories about everything."

"Unconscious?" I say. "Does he look any different?"

"Kind of," says Reni. "He's, like, taller, I think.
And maybe a little more Henderson-ish, if you know

what I mean. He says his confidence is up a few notches, which is going to make things impossible around here."

"Oh," I say, "did he mention anything about me?"

"You? No. Why should he? He says he's glad he went away. It's changed everything. He has already gotten two letters from Agarina."

"Agarina?" I say. "Does he, um, talk about her much?"

"Yeah," goes Reni, "he's all Agarina this and Agarina that. He's finished his novel. He's got one hundred and twenty pages written and it even has a 'The End' at the end. There was so much robot blood in the end, I had to skip a bunch of pages. I was, like, 'Barf bag, please.'"

"Oh," I say yet again, wishing there was some other word that would come out of my mouth, but *oh* describes it all, all the regret and mistakes on my part. *Oh* carries with it the empty sound of my own idiot head knocking against my own idiot inner brick wall. *Oh.*

"Hey, Agarina must be cool," says Reni. "She edited the book for Henderson and she cut out the story about the girl who had her foot stuck in the elevator. I was like, 'Thank you, there is a god.' Finally I'm not caught in Henderson's novel anymore."

"Oh," I say again. "Are they, um, dating?"

"It sounds like it," says Reni. "Honestly, I can't think anybody in the world would want to date *him*."

"Yeah," I go.

"It's weird. It's like thinking of your parents making out. You start thinking about it and then five letters pop into your mind. G.R.O.S.S."

I feel a terrible sadness. How can Henderson ever forgive me for being so stupid? Have I ruined everything? "Reni, I'm going over to Pottsboro Park. I need some air. I want to do some cartwheels. I *need* to do some cartwheels. It's been ages and ages and ages since I did any cartwheels. If you want to talk more, I'll be near the Bonnie Benton bench."

I can't really talk to Reni about what is happening inside my loony head. My own stupidity caused me to lose what I didn't even know I had. I was blindfolded, baffled, and blundering. I feel like an apple tree that was full to the top with apples and then someone came along and shook that tree and every apple came crashing to the ground. Every apple is gone out of my branches. And I am a four feet seven and one-eighth inches apple tree standing here with nothing in my leaves but wind. Wow. I wish I could tell Henderson that. He'd be like, "Hey, that's a good line." He says writing a good line is like coming across this uncut diamond waiting there in the gravelly earth. Wow. I couldn't talk about this with anybody but Henderson. I wish he hadn't gone away. No, I'm glad he went away. I don't know what I want. I don't know what I'm doing.

When I get to the park, I can't believe how green it is. The grass has that new-haircut, ears-sticking-out, fresh clean look about it. Henderson. Henderson. It will be good to run this out of me, to tumble and flip and do front tucks and aerials and handsprings, millions and trillions of them, until I'm so exhausted I won't feel this unbearable longing, this unbearable feeling of

I don't know what. If I have lost Henderson before I've even had him, then what will I do? Maybe I could get him back. I could have ten T-shirts made, saying things like HENDERSON, I DIDN'T SEE. I DIDN'T KNOW. Another one would say, HENDERSON, I LOVE YOUR NAME. I LOVE YOUR NOVEL. I LOVE YOUR FLANNEL SHIRTS, YOUR SMILE. I LOVE BENJAMIN FRANKLIN AND DINOSAURS AND VOLCANOES. I am a girl volcano doing hundreds and hundreds of cartwheels, and every time my feet go over my head, I feel like a flipping Ferris wheel. My world turns over and the park turns over and the sky and trees turn over. And I long to turn back what happened, the way it happened.

I do five more handsprings, five aerial cartwheels, and five backflips and by then I am so exhausted, I go over to the park bench and throw myself down

Agarina. Girl poet. Disguised stalker. Thief. Still, I'm the fool who didn't know her own heart. I close my eyes and let my hair fall back behind me. I look up at the sky. Unchanging forever sky, there above me always, even as my whole world collapses, turns over, changes, and shatters.

Suddenly, I notice there is a digital camera sitting on the park bench beside me. Weird, I'm thinking. Someone has lost a camera. I look around for anyone, but the park is empty. There is only wind here and trees blowing, and a kind of strange silence.

"Hello?" I call out. Well, if someone left a camera here, I should take it to the lost and found. Shouldn't I? I think about picking it up and then I finally do. It's a typical Canon digital, like ones I've seen around. Thinking maybe I can figure out who owns it by looking at a photo, I push the ON button. The wind in the trees roars around me, and the leaves sound like they are being washed clean with wind. The camera lights up. I hit the PLAY button, and a photo pops up on the screen. In the photo I can see someone is drawing a big heart on the cement with a piece of pink chalk. Underneath the heart it says *Thinking of you*.

I take a breath. I'm sort of trembling like the leaves around me. I hit the button, and the next photo appears on the screen. It shows someone again. I can't see a face, just hands and a torso. Someone is holding a huge bouquet of purple striped tulips. Underneath at the bottom of the photo, it says, *I picked these in winter for you.*

I hit the button again, and this time there are chocolates with the initials *JB* impressed on them, arranged in lines to make letters and words. The chocolates form the words *Miss you*. I close my eyes and bite my lip and then I open them and hit the button again.

In the next photo, someone is hidden behind a large piece of paper. On the paper it says, *I never had a job as a messenger for the assistant principal.* I hit PLAY again. *I came to South at lunch because I wanted to be with you.* I close my eyes again, and this time I start crying.

I can barely read what the next photo says. It shows just a torso of someone wearing a T-shirt. I have to push the ENLARGE button to see the letters clearly. Printed on the T-shirt are these words: THUMB, I HOPE I WILL NOT BORE YOU WITH HOW TOTALLY, TOTALLY I ADORE YOU. THE FUNNY WAY YOU HAVE OF TALK-ING, THE CUTE WAY YOU HAVE OF WALKING. PLEASE DO NOT FEEL THAT I AM STALKING YOU. LOVE, HENDERSON. My eyes are full of tears. They fall all over the camera and all over my hands.

I hit the PLAY button again, and the next photo shows someone hiding behind a large paper fan, and the note Henderson borrowed is pinned across the fan. It says, *I am your biggest fan.* Henderson. Henderson.

One more time I hit the PLAY button and there is Henderson wearing another T-shirt, and on this T-shirt it says, WILL YOU GO TO THE SPRING FLING DANCE WITH ME TOMORROW NIGHT?

I look around the park. Nothing moves but the leaves in the trees, sighing, cooing, whispering. I get up and run to the center of the green. I hold out my arms and I shout, "Henderson. Henderson. My answer is yes. Yes. Yes. Yes."

Chapter Thirty

By the time I get back to our condo building, it's getting dark. But it's a quiet, warm darkness, the kind of darkness that might be inside a soft flower bud just before it cracks open and blooms, the kind of darkness that is saving safely all sorts of things for tomorrow.

I go up the elevator, then decide to hit the ROOF button, and I push open the door to the night sky. The whole world is covered in a glittery dome of stars. I almost get scared looking up at them. Where do they begin and where do they end? What would the edge of the universe look like? Henderson has lots of theories about this. He ought to know. He's the one who owns a piece of the sky, his own meteorite, a falling star of his own. It came to him in a box from Iowa. But how many millions of miles beyond that had it really traveled? Like that song, *Catch a falling star and put it in your pocket*. Henderson.

I go downstairs and walk into our apartment. Grandma and Grandpa are playing Trivial Pursuit again. It's a close game. The question that just came up is "How long was John Lennon's hair on his first American tour?" For some reason, seeing them sitting there battling it out over this question gives me a nice warm feeling, like just for this moment, every star in every universe is in the right place.

When Henderson comes to get me the next night, I'm all ready. I'm wearing once again the green silk prom dress, which my grandma had cleaned and pressed for me while I lay sick in bed.

I hear noises outside our apartment, thumping and the sound of papers shuffling, and so I open the door to find my friend Henderson, owner of an eBay falling star, lover of astronomy, volcanoes, dinosaurs, old movies, rocks, Ben Franklin, new big words, robots, sushi, garbanzo beans, his own novels, and me. Me! He's maybe a little taller, maybe a touch goofier, but also more sure and happier. Why is he so happy?

"Hey, Thumb," he says.

"Hey, Hen," I go.

We ride the Toot Toot Tourist Trolley over to North Middle, and the whole way there, people keep taking our photograph. One lady calls out, "It's such a riot. He's so tall and she's so tiny. Are you going to a prom? Can I take a picture?"

On the trolley sitting next to me, Henderson gets out three candy bars from his pocket and says, "Pick your favorite, but I should warn you the PayDay bar is three weeks old." He puts his head against the glass window, where behind him all of South Pottsboro blurs by. As he leans his head back, he's watching me in the reflection in the windows opposite us. It feels nice to have a reflection of somebody looking at my reflection like that. "You finished your novel?" I say.

"Yeah, do you want to hear the ending? "

"Duh," I say. "You needed to ask?"

Writers always seem to carry with them various samples of their work. Ask any one of them. They are always ready to give a lengthy reading. Henderson unfolds a piece of paper from his flannel shirt pocket and begins to read to me. " 'Now, Rowan knew he was not a robot because when he bled, his blood was not blue. No, his blood was red. Rowan in the end was human. After all the suffering caused by all those menacing robots from planet Zing Zong, Rowan knew it was now possible to look directly at Zandra, Zandra the Princess of Jupiter, the one he had loved all his life. He reached out to take her hand. True, he was covered all over with scars and scratches and stitches, but then, in a way, so was she.' "

Henderson closes his eyes. I close my eyes. Then he says, "The end." And we both sit there lost in Henderson's novel.

•　　•　　•

I do think my mother would have liked Henderson. And I would have liked to introduce him to her, but then, I am just introducing myself to her after forgetting so much for a whole year. In a way, I can feel her presence tonight. In the boat on Lake Mescopi, she told me she would always be with me in my heart no matter what happened, and she is.

As proof of that, when we get to the Spring Fling Dance, I find the theme is Stars and the song they are playing in different variations is "Oh Stars in the Sky." You might think, "No, no, it can't be. It's too strange." But my grandma would say, "Strange? I think not. Coincidences are the marvelous little mysteries of life. Don't question a coincidence. Just enjoy it."

The Spring Fling Dance takes place on the green, grassy-smooth football field, and it's strung with lights that look like stars and there are banners with galaxies and spinning planets painted on them. When night falls, the real moon and stars will be above us. Maybe we'll even see a shooting star or a cluster of falling stars dropping down the horizon to land somewhere in Iowa.

Henderson says, "Thumbelina, you didn't wear the crown of flowers."

"Oh, I lost it," I say, "on Cinnamon Street."

"I guess I brought you something, then," he says and he reaches in his pocket and gets out the headband with reindeer antlers sticking up along the top, and he puts it on my head. "There's your crown, Thumbelina," he says. Then he reaches in his pocket again and presses the meteorite into my hand. "You know I found out something interesting," he says. "Benny McCartney got a job as a pizza delivery boy on the very day I bought this piece of falling star. The very moment the eBay auction ended and the falling star was mine, Benny signed on with Palomeeno's Pizza."

"How do you know that?" I say.

The Hen smiles. "I have my ways," he says.

I stare up at Henderson and he looks one minute handsome and brown-haired and dark-eyed and tender and the next second he looks a little awkward and then a split second later he's part nerd or geek and a little shy and then sooo handsome and sure again, and I'm thinking what my grandma said to me: "Oh, we're all complicated. Every prince is ten percent nerd. No one is nerd free. It doesn't work that way. But we are all beautiful, each one of us." How does my grandma know everything? (Well, almost.)

I look up at Henderson. He's my Frosty the Snowman and he has his arm around me and his hand on my waist at my back and it feels so warm. He looks down at me and he kisses me with his eyes. And with my eyes I kiss him back, and it feels better than any real kiss anybody ever had.

Oh stars in the sky,
All the stars twinkling by,
I wish and I sigh
At the stars so high.
I wish and I sigh
And I wonder why.
Why? Why? Why?

They say that true love always brings with it great and generous acts. Sometimes, amazing things happen to people and nobody knows about it. Nobody knows or cares. Someday many years from now in the faraway future, I will look back and say, "That year when I was in seventh grade, I knew a boy named Henderson Elliot, and what he did for me was extraordinary and who he was and how he won my heart was nothing short of incredible."

Some people in peril don't get saved, like Marty Hoey or my mom, and some people in peril do get saved, like me. Maybe it *was* because Henderson bought a chunk of a falling star, a gold-flecked quiet and ever-hopeful star. I hold it now tightly in my palm.

Author's note

I was eleven years old when my father took his own life. Before that, my world had been beautiful, like Louise's. I had friends, a school, violin classes, and a close-knit family. While our stories are quite different in many ways, after learning of my father's death, I too became very sick with a high fever for a week or so. When I awoke I was so weak, I had to relearn how to walk. I soon found myself in a frozen landscape. I avoided all contact with any part of my old life. In fact, I asked my mother to help me change schools so that I wouldn't have to face my old friends. I never played the violin again and it took me some time to find my way out of my own winter storm.

I am told many children block out the memory of trauma. In fact, the healing process can only truly begin when we are willing to remember.

Acknowledgments

A very special thank-you to my wonderful and insightful editor, Rachel Griffiths, dear friend, who helped me find my way through the thickets and fields of this story. Also special thanks to Arthur Levine. What a joy it is to be a part of the Arthur A. Levine Books family! (Thank you, Mallory Kass.) And thank you to all the incredibly nice people at Scholastic, especially Nikki Mutch, Sue Flynn, Becky Amsel, Whitney Lyle, Cheryl Weisman, Jana Haussman, and Ann Marie Wong.

I am also grateful to my friends Yvette Feig and Bob Murray, who read the book aloud together on their one-week vacation this year. Thank you to my kind readers, Kristy Carlson; Mary Swanson; Linda Smith; Sarah Wesson; Jillian Fay, gymnastics coach; and my sister, Marcia Croll. I am forever grateful to my poet mom, Ruth Stone, who has heard this book at least twice and who always laughs over and over again in all the right places. And thank you to my husband, ever-patient David Carlson, who by the way, has saved my life three times!